I0739364

A Space Between

A Novel

Ranjita Ghosh

ISBN 978-0-9948378-0-6

Cover Design: Andrea Mendis

To the Ghoshes,
especially one named Sudip

Contents

Chapter One

The sound was incessant. Daniel couldn't tell where it was coming from. But there it was, ringing and ringing and buzzing and buzzing. He tossed and turned, willing the device to free itself from its deafening counterpart. But it soldiered on, as if its singular purpose on the planet was to prevent Daniel from achieving peace.

A newly tanned arm reached over a horizontal and fidgety Daniel. A warm body followed the arm and suddenly the noise stopped. It finally dawned on him to open his eyes. The light was far too zealous. It engulfed him and overwhelmed him and he squeezed his eyes shut again. That sudden motion resulted in his head throbbing. He lifted his hands to his temples and rubbed them. *What the heck happened last night?*

"Good morning," he heard a murmur next to his ear and a felt faint wisp of breath.

Oh.

Daniel decided to endure the light and open his eyes once more. He turned his head to the left and his eyes widened. A beautiful woman lay next to him with a still, seductive smile. The recollection of the evening before started to dawn on him. The party. The nightclub. The tequila. Oh, the tequila. Oh, the dancing. Oh, the girl. His younger brother Paul had turned twenty-nine the night before, and in keeping with tradition, Paul had an all-out to-do on the actual day. In this case, a Thursday night. Bad idea. The party had been a success, and Daniel had definitely met plenty of interesting people, but being the only sibling of the birthday boy implied he was required to drink as if it was his own birthday. Or as if he was twenty-one again.

The night had gone from crazy to crazier as Paul had a plethora of single lady friends. They were all fascinated with the taller, slightly better looking, but more mysterious version of Paul. The two brothers were quite popular amongst the female crowd. Their dirty blond hair, intense blue gaze, and natural confidence caused heads to turn whenever they walked into a bar, especially if they were together. Daniel's features were softer than Paul's. His eyes were slightly rounded at the edges and his jaw was not as square as his brother's. These small differences had always made him appear friendlier and more approachable,

Daniel couldn't recall what had happened after three of the ladies managed to push him onto the dance floor. Before he knew it, the next morning had arrived. Apparently one of them, or who he thought was one of them, was sleeping under the same covers as him.

"Hi," Daniel managed to find his voice. He pushed himself up onto his elbows and looked around. He was relieved to find that he was at least in his apartment. No walk of shame today. Daniel leaned on his elbows and gazed around the unit, as if staring at it for the first time.

He was happy with his choice of apartments. He had scoured twenty-three different condos and lofts in the downtown area before finally settling on his current habitat. It was a gorgeous 750 square foot apartment with a view of the CN Tower and the Air Canada Centre. It had one bedroom and one bathroom but that was all he needed at this point in his life. His close friend Abigail had helped him furnish the place, giving it a sleek style with random vintage accessories for character. Abigail was all about the vintage accessories, and forgave the fact that Daniel had chosen to live in the corporate yuppie part of downtown, instead of the hipster part where she resided. Right now, the gorgeous mid-twentieth century armchair that she presented to him as a housewarming gift was covered with clothes. Several of which, were not his own.

The stranger arose from the bed as well, the white bed sheet draped strategically over her. She smiled again. This time it seemed sweeter, although in his hazy post-tequila state he wasn't sure if anything was as it seemed.

Daniel rubbed his eyes and attempted to figure out the next non-machismo thing to say. He smiled at her first, to appear less creepy.

"So, good morning," he said. *Brilliant.*

She grinned. "It's okay. I can appreciate the awkwardness of this moment."

He nodded, his head still throbbing. He opened and closed his eyes several more times hoping that would help his somewhat blurry vision. He didn't wear glasses or contacts, so there was nothing else he could think of doing to focus his eyes. He needed *Aspirin* and lots of it, he thought to himself. And water. Why wasn't there a glass of water on his nightstand, like in all the television shows he watched? He actually glanced at his nightstand to see if water would magically appear, but then noticed his alarm clock. The neon numbers shone back at him: 8:43.

Daniel's throat let out a hoarse yelp as he jumped out of bed.

"Oh my God!" He scrambled around the room, not really doing anything in particular. He picked up random articles of clothing from the floor and started tossing them arbitrarily over his shoulder.

"Hey!" the girl protested. "That's my dress!"

Daniel looked up from his harried state and noticed the girl properly for the first time. She was gorgeous. That was a given. Daniel Harp didn't just bed anyone. Even with the typical morning-after look, her hair shone and her eyes sparkled. This was all great, but it was now 8:44 which meant he had sixteen minutes to shower, change, and run to the office to meet his boss for what had already been referred to as a career-changing meeting. Of course, he also had to figure out how to remove another human being from his bed without resorting to anything physical. It might have helped if he remembered her name.

"Sorry," Daniel said. He gently tossed the dress over to the girl. "Listen, last night was a lot of fun and I hate to do this, but I am really late for a meeting." He watched her as she started to pull the dress over her head. "I know it sounds cliché, but it's true. I swear."

The girl slowly got out of the bed and nodded.

"I understand, you really don't have to worry about it, Daniel."

Dammit, Daniel cursed to himself. She remembered his name. Figures, since she probably had her eye on him from the start of the evening.

"Great," he continued. "Do you need me to call you a cab or anything?"

"Nope, I'm good. There are plenty of cabs outside, waiting to take people home from their one-night stands."

Daniel smiled in spite of himself. Good, he thought. At least we're on the same page about that. Daniel watched as she found her shoes near the doorway and put them on carefully. She pulled her hair back in a loose ponytail as she wandered around looking for what he could only deduce was her purse.

Wow, she really is pretty, Daniel thought. On any other day, he would have stayed and chatted with her, and then eventually figured out how to find out her name casually. But, not today. His boss was waiting.

Sure enough, she found her purse under a pile of clothes on Abigail's armchair and headed towards the door.

"Thanks for a lovely night," she said smiling. Daniel followed her to the door, dressed only in a white t-shirt and boxers.

"And you as well," he added. He gave her a quick kiss on the cheek and she walked out the door.

Daniel closed it behind her and stood there for a minute. Why did he keep doing this? He usually felt like crap afterwards, and he was never sure why. He was young, successful and single. This is what men of his age did, although it never quite felt right. It all seemed so superficial and shallow. Sure he had a great night, or at least he thought he did. Sigh, he didn't even remember it. What was the point in engaging in something that he couldn't even recall as a memory? For the sheer instant pleasure in exactly that given moment? Maybe. Maybe not.

His brother Paul on the other hand had found the love of his life, Megan, at the age of twenty-four. He had stayed fully committed to Megan and was planning on proposing soon, on their five year dating anniversary. Sometimes Paul mentioned in passing, how he felt he was missing out on the young, hip, single lifestyle that his brother led. But Daniel knew deep down inside that Paul had achieved a level of contentment that he was still searching for.

A creak in the apartment jolted Daniel out of his thoughts and he remembered the time again. *Dammit,* now he was down to fourteen minutes.

He quickly jumped in the shower and hoped that his face was clean-shaven enough for work. He ran to his closet, found a clean shirt and a pair of pants and started hunting for his shoes. Being a typical guy, he had only one pair of black shoes and one pair of brown shoes. He needed his black shoes right now, which, of course, he wore last night and couldn't remember where he had taken off in his drunken stupor. Brown shoes meant he would have to change his entire outfit. Feeling more like a girl than he cared to imagine, he quickly changed into a tan shirt and green pants and found his brown leather belt and shoes to complete the ensemble.

He grabbed his keys and wallet from his antique console (another Abigail find), threw his laptop bag over his shoulder and ran out the door. "Hold the elevator!" he yelled, to no one in particular.

***

With two minutes to spare, Daniel found himself on the elevator heading up to his office. Days like this, he was glad he made the decision to move closer to work. His office building was at the corner of Bay and Adelaide, the financial hub of the city. It was a standard glass-embossed, seventy-eight story monstrosity that mocked the smaller buildings around it. It couldn't appear more corporate if it tried. The building was abuzz with the usual morning chatter and excitement for the weekend that was coming up.

Daniel strode out of the elevator and nodded at the receptionist on the way to his cubicle. Having worked in Information Technology all of his adult life he had gotten used to the fact that software departments preferred an open, collaborative environment with low cubicles and desks aplenty. Even though he currently worked for a relatively stuffy financial services company, his department had kept the young, vibrant creative atmosphere that all good website employees required. Daniel threw his jacket on this chair, placed his laptop on his desk and headed directly to his boss's office.

"Hey, Steven," Daniel said as he planted himself in Steven's guest chair. His boss was the assistant vice-president of the web department, which granted him an office with a large window and a mahogany desk. Heaven forbid the senior management sat amongst the commoners.

"Daniel, how are you? You look terrible." Steven looked up from his laptop and leaned back in his plush, leather chair. "Let me cut straight to the chase," Steven continued, before Daniel could defend himself. "As you know, our web presence on the market has been growing exponentially. Our customers demand more features on a more regular basis. We haven't been able to keep up with that demand, which is something I'm not willing to accept."

Daniel nodded. Having been a project manager on most of these new features for the last two years, he was well aware of the department's limitations.

"We're thinking of outsourcing some of the easier development work, to free up our folks so they can start thinking more innovatively and begin developing a strategic roadmap of new enhancements."

Outsourcing, Daniel thought. Ugh. He had worked in the industry long enough to wonder when it was his department's time to go this route, and now it had arrived. He had heard horror stories from peers in similar situations and was always wary of when his day would come.

"What do you think?" Steven interrupted his thoughts.

Daniel hesitated. He had worked under Steven for eight months now, and found him to be an honest, straightforward boss. Both men were succinct in their speech, and both were professional in all manners, but where Daniel liked to occasionally throw in the odd joke, Steven kept things serious and sober. One thing Daniel could commend Steven on was being mindful of others, especially his team. Regardless of anything that was pushed down on Steven from the top of the corporate ladder, he was always willing to have an open discussion with his staff. Because of that, Daniel felt he could be forthcoming with him.

"To be frank Steven, I haven't heard the most flattering things about the whole process. I understand it can be very time-consuming, and I'm not sure the pros outweigh the cons."

Steven nodded thoughtfully. "I've heard similar rumblings. But I believe it is because the process is never initiated in the best manner. Having said that, I had an idea I wanted to run by you."

Daniel leaned forward in his chair slightly. "Go on," he said, not sure where this was leading.

"I want to send you to India, to help kick start the process with the new employees that will work for us."

Daniel raised one eyebrow and gulped at the same time, a bizarre reaction to a seemingly more bizarre request. India? "How long?" Daniel asked first.

"I'm thinking initially for six months, and then perhaps a couple of smaller trips before the end of the year."

Daniel exhaled slowly. His brain was attempting to process the news. India for six months? He had never traveled anywhere for six months. And India? He wasn't sure if saying the country's name over and over in his head was helping the situation. Wasn't it hot, and polluted, and hot? On the other hand, this was a huge responsibility that Steven was bestowing on him. He could have asked any of the other project managers. Heck, they even had an Indian guy in their office. But he had asked Daniel. He couldn't turn this down. Could he?

"What do you think about that?" Steven asked.

Daniel let out a slight mouthful of air. "I'm not sure exactly," he continued slowly. Truthfully, Daniel was hoping to have gotten the recognition without the extended trip to a third world country halfway around the planet. He was flattered that he was being held responsible for such a massive initiative. And he knew that any future job he wanted would look very highly on this new global experience. *But India*? Couldn't it have been a slightly less congested country?

"Daniel?" Steven interrupted his thoughts again. "I want you to take some time to think about it. Of course we would try and find a six month period that suits your schedule as much as possible."

"I appreciate that," Daniel said, finding his words again. "Steven, I'm flattered that you're asking me. I really am. But, what exactly would you need me to do there?"

"To be honest, we haven't worked out all the details. But this is what we know so far. We've had a few recruiters on our side hire a small team of web designers working out of the IT Sector in Kolkata, India. They are led by a man I, myself have hired, Sunil Ray, the project manager for that specific group. He would be responsible for prioritizing, budgeting and making sure that the features are completed by his team."

Daniel nodded. This all sounded relatively easy, so why the six month business trip?

Steven continued. "As you know, our processes at TargetLife are a little different. We've worked hard to fine-tune an extremely well thought out and nuanced business procedure that gets our projects completed on time. This plan is hard to teach over the phone and online. We find it best if there are multiple in-person meetings."

"Why wouldn't you just bring Sunil over here where I can train him?" Daniel inquired.

"We thought about that, but then decided that it would be a good idea if you met the entire team personally. We need them to feel associated with our department and nothing helps than a face to face meeting."

Daniel nodded. He couldn't disagree with Steven. Even their own department was split between Toronto and Guelph, a university city an hour west of Toronto, and he found himself willing to travel happily between the offices to keep the lines of communication open.

"Well Steven, I can definitely see the benefits of this new process."

"Look Daniel, I know it's a lot to ask. And we can compromise on a few things." Steven got up from his chair and came around to lean against the front of his desk, his usual 'let's talk openly' pose. "For example, if after four months you find that the team is doing great on their own and Sunil has really picked up our little eccentricities of project management, then I would be fine with you heading home early."

Steven crossed his arms over his chest. Daniel had worked with Steven long enough to know that this was his 'this is the best I can offer you' stance.

Daniel wasn't sure how many more times he could nod his head and say he appreciated the opportunity. So he took this as his cue to end the meeting.

"Steven, I'll have an answer for you soon if that's okay."

Steven nodded. "Absolutely." He then awkwardly extended his hand out, and Daniel even more awkwardly shook it, something he hadn't done since he first met Steven.

Wow, Daniel thought. He really wants me to run with this initiative.

Steven released his hand and moved away from his desk, towards his office door.

"I really want you give this the proper amount of thought. We would be supporting you in any way you needed."

Daniel moved towards the door as well, headed into the hallway and turned back to face Steven.

Steven looked at him. "I've been to India, Daniel," he said quietly. "I know it sounds daunting and scary and might appear like a different planet. But I can assure you. If you let it in, if you let all of it in: the noise, the people, the colors, the life, you will love it. You will fall in love with it."

Daniel had never heard Steven use the word love before. It sounded strange coming from him. The general stoic presence of Steven made Daniel believe he didn't even know what love was.

"I'll let you know my answer as soon as possible," Daniel reiterated, deciding it was best to ignore the discussion about love.

Steven gave him a curt nod and closed his office door.

Daniel stood there for a moment again, much like earlier in the morning when his nighttime guest had left his apartment. He hadn't known then what the day would hold in store for him. Looking at his boss's glass door, he realized he still didn't know.

***

Two days later, on a gorgeously bright October afternoon, Daniel waited patiently for his brother on the street in front of his apartment building. The bright sun of midday glimmered on the car and even Daniel's designer sunglasses couldn't deter the glare. Paul lived three blocks away from Daniel, at Front and Spadina, in a new condominium steps away from the Rogers Centre, the home of the local baseball team.

It was their bi-weekly visit to their parents' house, and since Daniel was the only brother with a car, it fell on him to do all the driving. Not that he minded. Paul's driving skills were something left to be desired.

Daniel took the time waiting in the car to ponder his

conversation with his boss. Steven had told Daniel to think about the proposal over the weekend and get back to him on Monday. Well Monday had almost arrived and he was no closer to a decision. He had no idea what was holding him back so much. If anything, he had been in such a funk lately, that perhaps this was exactly what he needed to get his mind off of things - to get his mind off of her. Daniel sat there for a moment, engulfed suddenly by three years' worth of memories. He shook his head, as if he could literally make the thought of her fall out of his mind.

The passenger door opened and Paul slid into the seat holding an apple cinnamon pie. Paul was always in charge of dessert primarily because of his unhealthy obsession with anything sweet. He blamed it on his mother, who clearly missed having a daughter and needed to bestow her baking knowledge on someone. Daniel was in charge of the wine, having a fabulous collection that was also kick started by his mother. Daniel sometimes wondered what his father thought of his sons' interests in dessert and wine. Fortunately for him, they were also up to speed on the latest hockey developments.

"Did you make a decision about the job?" Paul asked, as Daniel pulled his car out onto the main road.

"I'm definitely leaning towards a yes," Daniel replied as he merged onto the highway.

"I would think this would be an easy answer. Six months in an exotic country. You have no obligations tying you down here." Paul looked at Daniel slyly. "Or do you?"

"Of course not. You know everything that happens to me in every waking moment of my life. I just think it's a big commitment. I want to make sure I fully understand all the consequences."

"What consequences? You're most likely going to get promoted as soon as you return here, you get to live in a five-star hotel with actual servants and from what I can tell, the work they're asking you to do is not rocket science. You're training a bunch of people on stuff you already know. Stop hesitating and accept the damn offer!"

Daniel didn't respond, and instead focused his gaze on the road.

"Wait a second," Paul peered over his sunglasses at Daniel. "You don't think she's going to come back to you do you?"

Daniel continued to stare at the road.

"Unbelievable! You're afraid to leave the country because you actually think she might try and contact you. Daniel – *you broke her heart!*"

Hearing Paul say it aloud made Daniel's breath catch in his throat. Oh how he wished he wasn't the one driving right now. All he wanted to do was close his eyes and rest his head back.

Paul sighed. "Look I'm sorry. I didn't mean to blurt that out. I just think these six months will do you some good. Help clear your head."

Daniel knew that Paul was right. He was always right - it irked him. Instead of admitting this, Daniel turned up the volume on the radio, and they drove the rest of the way without speaking.

By the time the brothers arrived at the Harp residence in St. Catherines, the sun was slowly beginning to set. It was a sleepy city, south west of Toronto. Daniel and Paul had grown up here their entire lives, moving only when they left to attend university – Daniel at the University of Waterloo, and Paul at the University of Western Ontario. St. Catherines boasted about its population, making it the largest area of the Niagara Region. Daniel had loved living here. He always felt that once he settled down, got married and had kids, he too would raise them in a place like this. His parents still lived in the same house that

the boys had grown up in, and had no plans to move to Florida like
their fellow retirees.

Daniel and Paul made their way into the modest sized house –
a lovely charcoal gray brick building with white shutters and white
railings. Their mother, Sophia, had spent most of their childhood
planting numerous shrubs and flowers to create an oasis of a landscape
in front of the house. In more recent years, the front of the house had
been recently re-done. The small lawn was now replaced with bright red
mulch containing a flow of river rock stones in the shape of, ironically, a
river. Sophia's original garden was now enhanced by a low retainer.
Containing brightly colored flowers and a brilliant lush tree in the
center, Daniel stood impressed at the sight. The original concrete
walkway was now a sand colored interlocking weave of patio stones.
There were no longer signs of the tire skid marks in front of the porch,
where both brothers would halt their bikes, leap off precariously and
run inside for dinner. The potted plants that used to sit by the front
door, a location that was trampled many a time by the numerous
adolescents that stormed through the house, were finally removed and
replaced with a wrought iron park bench. Daniel lamented at the irony
of how a bench would have been far more useful in his youth than the
plants with the complicated names he still couldn't recall. Daniel
remembered how his mother would often ask for help to water the
plants, and how he always flatly refused – too busy playing with friends
or watching television. Nevertheless, the garden thrived, and Daniel felt
a little pang of guilt every time he walked by it now.

But mothers were mothers, and forgiveness was their most
fervent trait. He became conscious of this fact every time he came
home and his mother wrapped him in a warm embrace. This day was
no different. Sophia Harp always had plenty of love to bestow on both
her sons.

The dauntingly, stern patriarch of the family, Richard, headed down the stairs, greeting his sons as if they had already disappointed him in some way. He was 6'4, three inches taller than his tallest son, and it was in these three inches where his dominance lay. Even though both boys were successful, Richard's approval was always out of reach. It had been fourteen years, but Daniel could remember as clear as day, the look on his father's face when he spoke of leaving pre-med. His heart had not been it for so many months that the truth was inevitable. Daniel wanted to reexamine his university program and find a subject he could truly enjoy. Richard had been less than pleased at the news. Being the father of a doctor was a vivid dream for him, one that had been so close to reality. Daniel knew that even to this day, any mention of his job, successes or not, would always leave Richard feeling regretful.

Richard shook Daniel and Paul's hands fiercely, their standard greeting, and the four Harps headed into the kitchen.

"India?" Richard exclaimed a short whlie later. The family was seated at the kitchen table and had just started eating their dinner when Daniel had finally told his parents about the job opportunity.

"Yeah Dad, it's a pretty big deal that they're asking me." Daniel pushed his peas around on his plate, not feeling very hungry all of a sudden.

"I think it's fantastic," Sophia piped in. "We could even come and visit you."

"Let's not get too ahead of ourselves dear," Richard stated. "We'd need to get vaccinated in order to go there."

Daniel rolled his eyes. He was contemplating taking the job just to get away from his father for six months.

"Well I'm definitely going to come and visit. Take a couple of weeks off work and we can go travelling within the country." Paul smiled enthusiastically at Daniel.

"Are you going to go for sure?" Richard looked at his son. "I mean, can't they send you somewhere else instead? Maybe somewhere in Europe?"

"You mean somewhere where there are more white people?" Daniel replied back hotly.

"Daniel!" Sophia exclaimed, quick to defend her husband. "He didn't mean that, and you know it."

Daniel sighed. He hadn't even packed his bags yet and already he felt like he had more than enough baggage. Being back at the dinner table with the whole family always made him feel eighteen again, the age he was when he left for university. He knew Richard still saw him that way as well. Daniel stared at his family. They all had different expressions on their faces. His mother hopeful, his brother excited, his dad, well his dad always had the same stern look on his face.

Maybe Paul was right. Perhaps he did need to get away and start fresh. Everything that was bothering him about his current situation would still be here when he got back. Why was it considered so wrong to run away, even if just for a little while?

"I'm going," Daniel said quietly, to no one in particular. "I've made my decision."

Paul smiled at him, clearly having already planned his upcoming vacation in his head.

"We're going to miss you Danny, but I think you made a good decision," Sofia said smiling.

"Mom, you can always come and see me, once you get your shots." Daniel leaned over and kissed his mom on the cheek. He looked over at his father, who appeared to be smiling, or maybe just wincing.

Two hours later, Daniel and Paul were back in the car heading into the city. "When do you think you leave for India?" Paul asked.

"I actually don't know – Steven said he'd be flexible with my schedule, and now that I'm accepting the offer, I guess we'll sort out all the details."

"Well, I'm glad you're going. I really think you need this. The work alone should take your mind off everything."

Daniel nodded. The point of this trip was to elevate his career status and nothing more, and that was where he was going to focus his head for the next six months. He just hoped beyond hope, that his pained heart would follow suit.

Chapter Two

The sweat clung to Aahna's mid-riff as she sat in the rickshaw on her way to the first home of the day. The plain cotton sari that most maids wore was pulled tighter than usual and all of its fabric felt embedded into her skin. It was unbearably hot for a January morning, the high reaching nearly 100. She looked up at the sky as the rickshaw bumped its way over a pothole for the umpteenth time. Having ridden the bicycle and carriage contraption her entire life she still wasn't accustomed to the bumpiness of each ride.

The sun shone brightly on her face and regardless of how many times Aahna's mother had told her to stay out of the sun for fear of getting darker, she couldn't imagine a more glorious feeling than the penetrating rays.

"Make sure your shift ends at ten o'clock and be waiting for me at the corner," Sourav yelled back in Bengali to his sister, as he cycled around a moving vegetable cart. "I have a pickup at ten thirty for Mr. Chatterjee and he hates it if I'm late."

Aahna nodded, hoping her brother could see into his side-view mirror. The mirror had been rusted since he bought the rickshaw from a neighbor three years prior. She wasn't sure what Sourav could see, but she also had no inclination to raise her voice back at him.

The rickshaw came to a halt in front of a low rise apartment building, causing Aahna to jolt forward and then be pushed back in her seat. This was the usual morning ritual. She got out of the rickshaw and waved to Sourav, as he headed off to a nearby stand to start his day.

Aahna waited patiently at the gate for the superintendent of the building to let her in. He was an older, balding gentleman who never spoke to her, but merely unlocked the doors and stepped aside as she walked through. Aahna made her way around the cars in the tiny parking garage and headed up the stairs to the fifth floor apartment.

Briiiiing. Aahna smoothed her hair and straightened out her sari as she waited for the owner of the apartment to answer the door.

"Come in," Moumita Ray said after opening the door. The two ladies nodded at each other without making eye contact. Moumita was an average-sized woman with long black hair wrapped in a long braid. She was still dressed in her nightgown and slippers.

Aahna headed directly for the front hall closet. Her first task in every house was always to sweep the entire floor with the shortened straw broom all maids in Kolkata used.

Moumita's husband, Sunil suddenly appeared from the bedroom, stepping around her and heading into the kitchen for his early morning tea. Sunil was a man of only 5'6 inches, but he exuded a sense of control and quiet power that never appeared forced or unwelcome. With his early on-set graying hair and wire-rimmed glasses, he appeared far wiser and older than his thirty-eight years.

"What time should I expect you today?" Aahna overheard Moumita asking Sunil, as she swept under the kitchen table and around the six chairs.

"I won't be home until late tonight." Sunil cleared his throat. "The project manager from Canada is reaching here tomorrow and our team has plenty to complete prior to his arrival."

"What do you think about the company making this man come all the way just to oversee you?"

"He's not overseeing me." Sunil seemed to be trying to make his wife understand. "He's training us on multiple processes that are integral to our business. I think how our relationship pans out will go a long way in determining the future of the Kolkata division of TargetLife."

Aahna heard Moumita sigh. She did that often, usually when Aahna had forgotten to dust some random knick knack in the large hutch in the dining room.

The lady of the house exited the kitchen and looked through Aahna as she made her way to the bedroom. Aahna used that as her cue to head into the kitchen and continue sweeping.

Sunil was leaning against the stove, still sipping on his tea and looking deep in thought. He smiled at Aahna as she worked around him. "How is your mother?" he asked politely.

Aahna's face lit up at the mention of her mother. "She's doing well Sir, thank you for asking."

"You know, she was always my family's favorite."

Aahna nodded. Sunil told her this almost every day, as if to make up for his wife's disregard of their many servants.

"And you? How have you been?" He placed the teacup and plate in the sink and began washing his hands.

"I've been all right I suppose. All things considered." Aahna stayed squatting on the floor, gathering all the kitchen dust and debris into one smaller pile.

Sunil stepped closer to her and Aahna kept her gaze on his black rubber slippers.

"Your mother will find you someone different. She's a very determined woman. It obviously wasn't meant to be with that man."

Aahna looked up and pushed herself off the floor, her knees creaking as she found her balance. "Maybe it's a sign that I'm not ready to get married yet."

"No one's ever really ready for marriage. If they gave everyone a moment to stop and think about the absurdity of living with another human being for the rest of one's life, people would most likely run in the other direction."

Aahna chuckled quietly, hoping his wife wasn't listening to their conversation. Having known Sunil Ray her entire life, she felt like she could speak to him to on an equal level. She remembered when they were little, how he used to chase her around his family's grounds whenever she joined her mother at work. He was thirteen years older and had always treated Aahna no differently than his own little sister. She knew she would be eternally grateful for that.

"I can never remember. How many other houses do you clean?" he continued.

"I have two more *Sir*," Aahna said, suddenly remembering her status in this house. "I had a third house but the owners moved to Delhi."

"Does that mean after five o'clock you're free every day?"

"Yes Sir. I am usually done everything by four thirty." Aahna wondered where this conversation was going.

Sunil leaned against the counter again. "Our regular cleaner in my office recently quit. She's pregnant and her husband doesn't want her to work anymore. We have an opening."

"What would you need me to do? I've never worked in an office before."

"It's not really that different. The floors where all of the employees sit would have to be swept and mopped each day, and all the desks dusted. The garbage would have to be emptied and the dishes from the kitchen cleaned. Once a week we would need the interior windows washed."

Aahna noticed Sunil stop abruptly, probably realizing how dictatorial he sounded for a moment.

"It's not really that different than what you do here," he finished quietly, looking out the window.

Aahna didn't respond.

"Anyway, talk it over with your brother and mother. You would have to take a bus to get to the IT sector, but the company would pay that expense."

"It sounds possible," Aahna said. "It would be hard for me to say no to the extra money."

"That's what I assumed as well. Besides, you've seen me go to school, get married and maintain a house. It's only fair that you see me pretend to work now."

She smiled.

"If you're interested, we'll have you start next week. I'll let the office manager know of the new arrangements."

"Okay Sir. I should probably get back to work here."

"Yes. I have to head into the office now anyway." Sunil left the kitchen, leaving Aahna standing there alone.

A few seconds later Moumita was at the door. "The dust is making quite a nice home on my shelves."

"I'm coming," Aahna replied, attempting to hide her disdain.

When the end of her shift finally approached, Aahna headed outside to wait at the corner for her brother's rickshaw to arrive. She leaned against a brick building and watched as taxis hurtled past her. The husbands of the neighborhood had long since left for work, leaving any of the non-working wives to head into the bazaar to sort out the day's grocery shopping. She stood off to the side, staying out of their direct path. A bus passed by, leaving an immense cloud of black smoke in its wake. Aahna grabbed the end of her sari and covered her mouth and nose without thinking twice.

She pondered the job proposition Sunil had broached her with. Her family could definitely use the money, especially since her engagement with the local store clerk had broken off. She had hated disappointing her mother, but some things were out of her control. The store clerk realizing his true feelings for a frequent customer being one of them.

Aahna sighed, thinking of how lucky Moumita was. She was fortunate to be married to a man like Sunil, and she never even realized it. Her mother had said everything in their lives was already written; therefore girls like Moumita were pre-destined to marry a kind and caring man.

A few minutes later, Sourav pulled up to the corner, his rickshaw bypassing a taxi and a pedestrian by a few inches. As Aahna sat down on the plastic seat, she wondered was written for her.

***

The temperatures had still not cooled by mid-January, and Aahna found herself constantly dabbing her forehead with her sari. Everywhere around her, people who were normally used to an extreme tropical climate were cursing at the sky for such a short reprieve. Two months of pleasant days and cooler nights was all everyone she knew asked for, and this year, their wishes had not been granted.

Aahna had not been fortunate enough to nab a window seat on the bus, and she found herself standing, trapped between an obese, questionable smelling grandmother, and a pretty college girl a few years younger than herself. Aahna did not have the privilege of riding on a public bus often, as her travels were limited to the core city and her brother's rickshaw had proved sufficient. However, Sunil had promised her a bus fare for this office job and a bus fare she had received.

After forty-five minutes of stopping and starting, the bus arrived within the confines of the Information Technology sector, located in Salt Lake City, just outside the main hub of Kolkata. The area was filled with high rise offices sporting some of the biggest technology names in the world.

Aahna slid her way through the crowded bus's Ladies' Section and climbed down the stairs as dozens of IT employees fought their way onto the front of the bus. She made her way past a few buildings before arriving to her destination, glancing over at the building number and not bothering to look at the large TargetLife sign just below it. She knew the English letters wouldn't have made sense to her anyway.

Aahna made her way to the back of the building, headed in through a service door and began to climb the seven floors to the main office. As she opened the door onto the lobby of that floor she ran right into a person standing on the other side.

"Oof!" exclaimed a woman.

"Shibani?" Aahna asked, recognizing the voice. She peered around the door and found her new friend sprawled on the floor. She grabbed her hand to help her up. "The door wasn't that hard was it?"

"Perhaps if I had been prepared for steel heading towards my face I might have chosen to dance instead of fall."

Aahna laughed. "Did you just get here?"

"Yes, just starting my shift." Shibani straightened out her sari and picked up the wet cloth she was using to wipe the floors. "I swear I don't know if these people walk in mud all morning before heading into the office. Someone should follow them around all day with this cloth."

"If everything here was clean, you and I wouldn't have a job now would we?"

"Always the optimist," Shibani smiled. "So how are you enjoying the first few days here?"

"It has been interesting. Cleaning a place at the end of the day seems far different than cleaning one at the beginning."

"How so?"

"You can almost feel what everyone was doing all day. The spilled coffee, the gum wrapper that missed the waste basket, the dozens of balled up paper on someone's desk. As if you are experiencing these insignificant moments along with them."

Shibani looked at Aahna skeptically. "You certainly read into things."

Aahna smiled. Maybe she did read too much into things. Or maybe she was so bored with her own existence that she became fascinated by the goings on of people she had never met. It was times like this where she stopped and realized that her entire life was already laid out for her. And nothing about it looked appealing.

"Enjoy your shift," Shibani said, interrupting her thoughts. "Let me know if you find any pencils that speak to you." Shibani chuckled as she headed through the doors of the other office that shared the seventh floor.

Aahna made her way into TargetLife's main area. She walked over to the cleaning supplies closet and grabbed her bucket and cloths.

She loved this time of the day. The office was so peaceful, with usually only one or two people left, finishing up their work to meet a deadline. You could almost sense the hard work in the air. Although really, Aahna had no idea what the atmosphere in any office was like. She pictured what she had seen in the Hollywood movies. Of people rushing around, picking up phones, yelling to each other, making deals. But that was just her imagination. For all she knew, this office could be as quiet as a library.

Chairs were scattered all around the main area. She began by rolling them back to their respective desks, while glancing at the pictures on each one. There were established families, new babies, older couples, friends vacationing. Everyone's lives looked so fulfilled. That instance that was captured could tell so much about a life. Or maybe it was the opposite. Maybe as soon as the picture was taken, the friends had parted, or the baby had started crying. She wondered what people would think of her if she was ever caught on film. The only cameras she had ever seen were in the stores she passed on the way to her various jobs, or the ones that her employers locked up when she or her colleagues arrived for work.

A cough in the corner interrupted her thoughts. She looked up to see a man hunched over his desk, typing furiously on his laptop. His skin was incredibly fair, and Aahna noticed the blond hair. Ah, so this was the foreigner. She recalled Sunil and Moumita's conversation in the kitchen.

The man looked up just then and caught Aahna staring. She quickly put her head down and pretended to dust the picture.

She continued to look down until she heard typing again. Aahna lifted her head ever so slightly to glance at the man once again. He was still staring at his screen. Even from this distance, Aahna could see his bright blue eyes as they darted quickly from left to right, synchronized with the sound of the typing. His hair was slightly disheveled, the majority of it a straw color, with some hints of brown thrown in. His complexion appeared flawless, if only because he was sitting under the bright halogen office lights.

Aahna had seen white men before, wandering the streets of Kolkata with large backpacks and water bottles. Tourists were rampant in the city, everyone looking to find a spiritual side to themselves. That, or to appreciate how easy their lives were back home.

But she had never been alone with one. The stillness of the air and the clicking of the laptop made Aahna acutely aware of her surroundings. She wasn't fearful, but a slight anxiousness was coming over her. She abandoned the desk she was cleaning and headed into the kitchen to start tidying up there. Perhaps the gentleman would leave for the day before she would have to return to the main area.

Aahna began placing all of the dirty coffee mugs and plates into the dishwasher. As she leaned sideways to put down a fork, she noticed a pair of legs out of the corner of her eye. Aahna jumped.

"I'm sorry," the man said. "I didn't mean to startle you."

Aahna didn't say anything. She wasn't even sure she was supposed to turn around.

"You probably don't understand what I'm saying," the man continued.

She understood him just fine; she just had no idea how she was supposed to behave.

The man came into the kitchen and placed his coffee mug directly into the dishwasher. "One less thing for you to do," the man said.

Aahna kept her gaze down but she had a feeling the man was smiling. She wanted to look at him, if only out of curiosity. He was a foot away from her now, and the faint smell of cologne reached her nose. For some reason, it was intoxicating. She moved away from the sink slowly and turned sideways to face him directly. She looked up at him and realized she was right. He was smiling.

It was infatuating. His teeth were an impeccable shade of white, and his lips parted in the most flawless way. He was in one word, perfect. Aahna made up her mind that he rivaled any one of the actors she saw on magazine covers.

"My name is Daniel," he spoke.

If melted chocolate could turn into a sound, it would represent his voice. Aahna felt her knees weaken and she almost had to hold onto the counter for support. What was wrong with her?

"I don't know why I keep speaking, you have no idea what I'm saying," Daniel continued as he headed over to the fridge. "What does it matter? Even the people that do understand English here look at me like I'm crazy. It's like they're seeing my lips move and hearing a sound, but nothing is registering. You know what I mean?"

Aahna nodded in spite of herself. *Uh oh.*

Daniel closed the fridge door abruptly. "Did you just understand me?"

Oh God, Aahna thought. He's going to tell Sunil on me. Her claim to fame in her village will now be that the beautiful foreigner got her fired.

Daniel walked closer and peered directly at her with his blue eyes. "Why are you staying quiet?"

Aahna sighed. "I am so sorry, Sir. I did understand you. But only a little bit. I am sorry if I insulted you," she added quickly at the end. She cringed, waiting for the foreign man to lash out at her.

Instead he smiled. "That's impressive. I wouldn't have expected a person like you to understand English."

"Now who is insulting?" Aahna said hotly without thinking. Goodness. Had she gone crazy?

Daniel burst out laughing. "You're right, my apologies." He leaned against the counter next to her. In this position, she came up to his chest, and for a second she wondered what it would be like to lean against it. His left arm was a mere few inches away from her right hand.

Aahna noticed this and stepped away from him. She wouldn't want anyone to walk in and get the wrong impression.

Daniel didn't seem fazed. "So do you have a name?"

"Aahna, Sir."

"That's a very pretty name."

"I am sure you think that about a lot of the names you have heard here."

"Well don't tell anyone, but that's not actually true." Daniel flashed his smile again, and this time, Aahna smiled back widely.

Daniel appeared taken aback by this gesture. Aahna stopped smiling at once and walked further back.

"I have to continue working, Sir." Aahna looked away again, as she did when he first entered.

"Of course, I understand. I didn't mean to bother you." Daniel headed to the small entryway of the kitchen where Aahna had backed herself into. "It was a pleasure to meet you, Aahna." He said her name in almost a whisper and with that, he strode out of the kitchen.

Aahna stood there, almost frozen. She felt the weakness in her knees again and some kind of odd fluttering sensation in her stomach. She closed her eyes and heard him speak her name again in her mind. 'Aahna.'

Slowly she regained her composure and started filling up the dishwasher. But every so often, during the rest of the evening, she would close her eyes and hear his voice.

***

Riiing riing! Riiing riing! Daniel grabbed the hotel phone as he tucked in his shirt.

"Hey, it's Paul. Are you awake?"

"Yeah man, it's almost eight here. When are you going to get the time difference sorted out?" Daniel grabbed his laptop from the desk and shoved it into his bag.

"Probably when you're about to come back," Paul said. "So, how goes week three? Is it safe enough for us to visit?"

Daniel rolled his eyes. "You're not that immature are you?"

"Sorry," Paul said. "Seriously though, how goes it?"

"It's getting better. I'm adjusting slightly. At least the jet lag is completely gone now."

"And the work?"

"I think people are starting to get used to me being around. It was weird. First, they were treating me like some kind of God. Then they were treating me like an enemy. Now, they just ignore me and treat me like one of their own."

Paul laughed. "Good, the last thing we need is for you to come back with some sort of God complex. Anyway, I'll let you get to work. Listen I actually called because Megan and I sorted out our work schedules. We should be able to make it down there for a couple of weeks in March. Does that work for you?"

"Yeah that should be good. The weather will still be fairly hot, but it's not monsoon season or anything." Daniel looked around the hotel room for his cell phone and charger.

"Look at you sounding like a local," Paul said. "Anyway, Mom will probably call you later this week, and I'll send you the flight information as soon as we book it."

"All right – say hi to everyone for me."

"Yep, take it easy." The phone on the other end clicked.

Daniel put on his shoes and ran out the door for the elevators. He hated keeping the driver waiting.

The heat engulfed him almost immediately as he headed out the main doors of the lobby. After three weeks, Daniel still hadn't gotten used to the temperatures and he felt the sweat begin to surface on his forehead. He debated turning around and heading back into the air-conditioned hotel when he spotted the driver chatting with some of the hotel staff.

Daniel cleared his throat, and the driver jogged over to him.

"Sir, I am sorry to have you waiting," the driver said apologetically. His English was broken but understandable nonetheless.

"It's no problem, Mukesh," Daniel smiled. "I just need to get out of this heat."

"Of course!" Mukesh opened the rear passenger door and Daniel shuffled inside. He was certainly getting used to having a driver.

Mukesh pulled out of the Hyatt Regency's driveway and joined the other cars on the main highway leading into the city. Daniel braced himself for another zany car ride. He couldn't believe how fast and how close all these cars got to each other. He secretly prayed for his life each time driving was involved.

Daniel rested his head back and stared out the window as the car sped along the highway. The honking of the horns every twenty seconds deterred the journey from being even remotely peaceful. He passed by hundreds of people walking along the sides of the road with any animal you could imagine. Small huts dotted the edges of the paved road, and further down the embankment, hundreds of more huts could be seen. He witnessed fabrics of every possible color draped on clotheslines and people milling around carrying huge buckets of water. He was impressed with the ladies carrying straw baskets filled with bricks on their heads as they made their way from one area of the slum to another. Massive billboards appeared over the highway every fifty feet. Colored advertisements for everything from electricity, soap and clothing swam past Daniel's face, the models in the pictures looking nothing like the masses they were trying to represent. Some ideals are universal, he thought drily.

The road forked and the new high-rise office buildings came into view. They stood tall with a sense of arrogance, as if they couldn't be bothered to deal with the poverty a mere kilometer away.

Mukesh turned into the main part of the IT sector and drove into TargetLife's driveway.

"Here you go, Daniel Sir," Mukesh said, even though Daniel had asked him many times to not call him Sir.

Mukesh held the door open for him and Daniel waved quickly as he hopped out of the car and made a beeline for the building, trying to avoid the sweltering heat at any cost.

On the seventh floor, Daniel made his way to his corner desk. Employees smiled and nodded at him as he entered, and he heard the word "Sir" murmured more than once.

"Mr. Harp. Good morning," Sunil said, stepping out of his office.

Daniel had long since given up reminding Sunil that they were in fact, peers, and that 'Mr. Harp' was entirely unnecessary. Oh well, he might as well enjoy this level of respect as long as possible.

"Sunil, I thought you said January was supposed to be a cooler month."

Sunil chuckled. "It is, Sir, but apparently this year Kolkata wants to welcome you as warmly as possible."

"It's doing a fine job at that."

Sunil perched himself on the edge of Daniel's desk.   "Before I forget, my wife wants you to come over to our house tonight for dinner. She is already mad at me that you have been here for a few weeks and I have not extended the invitation. So please, spare me another argument with her and say you will join us this evening."

Daniel smiled, looking up from his laptop. "That's very nice of your wife. I'd be happy to attend."

"Excellent. I will call your driver and let him know you will be leaving with me tonight. We will leave around 6 o'clock."

Daniel nodded as Sunil left his desk. He watched Sunil head into his office, and then he turned back to his laptop and began to work.

It was five forty-five when Daniel felt he could finally stop typing. The day had turned out to be more hectic than he had originally anticipated, and he found himself feeling tired. Remembering his dinner plans, he headed into the kitchen to grab some last minute coffee for a quick jolt.

He heard the kitchen sink running as he walked in and Daniel found himself pleasantly surprised to see Aahna.

"Well, hello there," Daniel said, smiling brightly. He hadn't seen her since their first encounter several days ago.

Aahna turned around, not looking at him. "Hello, Sir."

Not again, Daniel thought. He grabbed a coffee mug and began filling up his cup. "Daniel, remember? My name is Daniel. You don't have to call me Sir. In fact, I insist."

Aahna nodded. "Yes, Sir."

Daniel gave up, wondering if he should just officially change his name in this country.

"So are you the regular, uh, cleaning person here?" What a stupid question, he thought to himself.

"Yes, I just started. I actually work for Sunil Sir and his wife."

"Oh you know Sunil!" Daniel exclaimed, happy to find a mutual topic of conversation. "He's a great guy!"

Aahna nodded again and turned back to the dishes.

Silence.

Daniel used the silence to look at Aahna carefully. She had struck him as beautiful from the moment he first laid eyes on her. He knew that if he had seen her on the street, she would have most likely blended into the crowd. But here, in the office, she stood out from all the rest of the staff he interacted with daily. He had only seen her smile once, but he hadn't forgotten it, having always been a sucker for a gorgeous smile.

"You never told me how you came to speak English," Daniel said, propping himself up against the counter so he could be right next to her.

"You never asked," Aahna replied softly. She didn't look up from the mugs and plates she ran under the water.

"I'm asking now." Daniel wasn't going to give up on this conversation that easily.

Aahna must have realized that as well, because she turned the water off and faced him. "If you must know, Sir, one of my former employers was an English teacher. He would test out his new lesson plans on me, and in the process, I learned to speak English. I cannot read or write it, but I suppose I can carry a conversation."

"Yes you can." Daniel flashed his smile at her.

Aahna blushed and looked away again. A smile crept up the side of her face and she looked like she wanted to say something.

When she didn't, Daniel continued. "I take it you normally don't engage in conversation with men like me."

"Engage?"

"Sorry, I mean I guess you don't chat with men like me often."

"If often means never," Aahna replied.

"Wow, and I always thought sarcasm was the hardest thing to teach." Daniel smiled.

"How do you like our city so far?" Aahna said, clearly ignoring Daniel's comment.

"It's been, um, interesting." Daniel hesitated, not wanting to insult her country. "To be honest, it's a little overwhelming. There are people everywhere!"

Aahna laughed. "We are a city of 17 million people."

"Did you know I tried to take a walk the other day? I almost got run over three different times, five different cars honked at me, and a rickshaw almost knocked me over into the side of a building."

Aahna continued to laugh.

"Stop laughing, it's not that funny," Daniel protested. "I swear a cow walked by me."

Aahna laughed even harder. "Don't be silly. We rounded up all the cows a few years ago."

"Well then, it would appear you forgot one." Daniel looked at Aahna, and found himself starting to laugh as well.

Aahna threw her head back, laughing while her body shook. Her dark brown eyes were glassy from the tears that were beginning to form. Daniel couldn't help but stare at her as she looked back at him in what he could only decipher was pure merriment.

She stopped laughing suddenly and their eyes fixated on each other. They both stood there in silence for a few moments.

"Mr. Harp?"

The voice appeared to come out of nowhere and both Daniel and Aahna jolted from their dream-like state.

Sunil was standing in the doorway. He didn't appear the least bit amused. "What's going on here?"

Aahna stayed completely silent, her back towards Sunil.

Daniel hopped off the counter. "Nothing Sunil, I was just chatting with Aahna here."

Sunil raised an eyebrow. Daniel suddenly felt the tension in the air. He could see Aahna's body stiffen and sensed her discomfort.

"We should get going," Sunil said coldly. He turned and walked away.

Daniel glanced back at Aahna. "What was that about?"

"You should go," she answered quietly.

"I don't understand. We were just talking."

"Please go, this does not look good," Aahna urged gently.

Daniel nodded feebly and walked away from her. As he left the kitchen, he wondered what she meant by 'this'.

Chapter Three

The ride to Sunil's apartment was relatively short in distance, but still took a good forty-five minutes with the never ending traffic congestion. Sunil appeared to have forgotten about the incident in the kitchen between Daniel and Aahna, as he was pleasantly chatty for the entire car ride. Sunil drove his own car into the parking garage, and the two men climbed the five flights to the apartment building. The door swung open as they arrived on the final platform and Moumita stood there welcoming them.

"Come in, come in," she smiled enthusiastically.

"Daniel, I would like you to meet my wife, Moumita," Sunil said as they were ushered into the foyer.

"Moumita, the pleasure is mine." Daniel smiled warmly and took her hand in his.   Moumita was over half a foot shorter than Daniel. She wore a silk sari that looked freshly pressed, and her hair was wrapped in a bun in the middle of her head.

"Ah yes, Mr. Harp. Welcome to our fine country." Moumita gestured towards the living room where they all sat down.

Daniel took in the quaint apartment. The furnishings were modest and comfortable, and the shelves were aligned with small statues and family photographs. There were several pictures of a young boy throughout the years. Daniel recognized the boy from a frame on Sunil's office desk – he was their seven-year old son, Alok. As if on cue, Alok bounded out of a room from the back of the apartment. He looked like a miniature version of Sunil with his large, kind eyes, slim build, and a dimple in the left cheek.

Upon seeing the tall, pale skinned stranger in his living room, Alok retreated behind his father.

"Alok, don't be shy," Sunil said. "Say hello to Mr. Harp from Canada."

Alok nodded, but didn't speak.

"Sorry about that," Moumita chimed in. "He needs to warm up to people first."

"It's not a problem. I'm assuming he understands English?" Daniel inquired.

"Yes, he's been attending an English medium-school since he was three years old. And Moumita and I try and speak to him in English as much as possible."

Daniel nodded. He was glad that he could speak easily with both of his hosts. Their English, although accented, was almost flawless. He was surprised to notice that their vocabulary was even more established than his own. Being raised in a British school system would do that to a person, he thought.

"Alok, why don't you finish your schoolwork and we will call you for dinner," Moumita said.

Alok nodded, smiled at Daniel, and then headed back to his bedroom. As he left, a woman dressed very much like Aahna stepped out of the kitchen with a tray of small plates filled with food. She placed the platter on the coffee table and stood back without saying a word.

"Mr. Harp, please have some samosas and fish cutlets," Moumita said, as she took a plate and hanced it to her guest.

"Oh wow," Daniel said. "This is a lot of food, but thank you." He took a bite of the samosa. "This is delicious," he said genuinely.

"I've eaten these before in Toronto, but this just has a whole different taste to it."

"I'm glad you like it," Sunil said. He nodded at the girl that had brought out the food and spoke quickly in Bengali.

She nodded back and keeping her eyes down, headed back into the kitchen.

Daniel watched her leave, and for a moment, found himself thinking of Aahna, wondering if she was still working in the office.

"Do you mind if I ask you something?" Daniel started.

His hosts nodded encouragingly.

"Exactly how many servants do you have?"

Sunil and Moumita both started laughing.

"We have a few," Sunil said. "She," he gestured towards the kitchen, "takes care of our food. We have another one that comes to clean our bathrooms every day, one that sweeps and dusts in the afternoon, and a couple more that take care of groceries and laundry."

Daniel leaned forward in his chair, fascinated. "Why would you not just have one person do everything?"

"Different people have to be responsible for different parts of the household. The person that cleans our bathroom can't make our food."

"Why not?"

Sunil appeared slightly embarrassed now. "Because," he said slowly, "the people who clean the bathrooms are considered the 'untouchable' class."

"That actually exists?" Daniel inquired.

"Yes, of course. It has existed for centuries."

"Should we not have evolved past all of that by now?"

"Mr. Harp, with all due respect, this isn't something that can be explained and understood over one meal."

Daniel took that to mean Sunil had no desire to continue this line of questioning, and even if further questioned, he would most likely repeat what his own parents had taught him.

Moumita had been glancing back and forth between the men during the exchange and now spoke up. "Mr. Harp, have you met many people at work?"

Sunil appeared relieved for the change in topic.

Daniel turned to focus his attention to Moumita. "Why yes I have. Everyone has been quite nice to me. I ever had the pleasure of meeting Aahna."

Sunil coughed suddenly on his fish cutlet.

"I'm sorry, who?" Moumita asked.

"Aahna," Daniel repeated. "I believe she works for you and Sunil, even though I noticed that you didn't mention her when speaking about your other staff." He could have sworn he caught Sunil wincing slightly.

Moumita raised an eyebrow and leaned back in her chair. "That is interesting." She looked over at Sunil, who appeared to be wishing he was anywhere but in this living room at this very moment.

Daniel looked at his two hosts suspiciously. "Is there something I should be aware of?"

Moumita and Sunil glanced at each other again.

"Look, Mr. Harp, I did not want to say anything." Sunil set down his plate of food. "It is not entirely appropriate that you interact with Aahna, especially how you were earlier today."

"What happened earlier today?" Moumita pressed. Her face had gone from pleasant host to critical elitist in a matter of seconds.

Daniel looked at her in surprise. Now he didn't like where this questioning was going.

"Listen, I'm not naïve," Daniel started. "I can appreciate the class and caste systems here. I have no desire to disrespect anyone. But I was merely having a nice conversation with Aahna. She seems to be a nice girl, that's all."

"She is a nice girl," Sunil said. "But Mr. Harp, there is a certain decorum that needs to be maintained. A senior representative from a foreign office cannot be seen socializing with a servant girl."

"Maybe he picks it up from you," Moumita responded coldly.

"What is that supposed to mean?"

"Oh please, you think I've never noticed your morning chats?"

"Moumita, first of all, I have known Aahna her entire life. And we are inside our apartment. The situation is completely different."

"It doesn't mean I have to be happy about it."

"We will discuss this later," Sunil said firmly to his wife. "Why don't you go check on dinner now?"

Moumita looked like she wanted to say something. Instead she got up and stormed out of the living room.

Daniel sat quietly. He had long since finished his plate of snacks, but was now wishing there was more food just to give him something to do.

Sunil stared at the floor in front of him.

They both sat in silence for a few minutes.

"I'm really sorry," Daniel said, finally breaking the stillness. "But, I don't really understand what just happened."

"It doesn't concern you. And I'm sorry you had to witness all of that."

"Is me chatting with Aahna really this much of an issue?"

"I've known her my entire life. She's a sweet girl, and I am a little afraid that if you pay too much attention to her, she will get the wrong impression. Do you know what I am trying to say here?"

"Oh. Yes, of course," Daniel nodded. "I don't think I've given her that impression yet, but I think I understand where you're coming from."

"Good. I would hate for her mother to come after me asking about your dowry expectations."

Daniel looked perturbed.

"I was joking," Sunil smiled. "But in all seriousness, I don't want you to think that we are being discriminatory. There is a just a certain way things are done here. And you should be remembered for the work you're helping us with, and not for fraternizing with the wrong person."

Daniel nodded. He had never been told whom he could or couldn't speak to, but he was in a different country now and had to abide by the rules.

"Great, so now that that is all cleared up, wasn't that interview with the new developer horrendous? Sometimes I wonder if these candidates have ever spoken to another human being before arriving."

Daniel laughed along with Sunil, but for some reason he felt a slight uneasiness in the back of his mind. He wasn't sure why it bothered him that he wasn't allowed to speak to Aahna. After all, he barely knew her. Maybe it was just loneliness but he had enjoyed her company, however fleeting.

As the two men continued to chat, Daniel noted the irony of his situation. Sunil had seemed worried about the impression that Daniel might have left on Aahna, but all Daniel could think of was the impression she had left on him.

***

The bus lurched to a halt and Aahna maneuvered her way down the narrow stairs to the side of the street. She hoisted her bag onto her shoulder and began her one mile walk from the bus stop to the small house where her family lived. The sun was slowly setting, and the majority of village residents were also heading home after a long day's work. Kids were playing a make-shift soccer game in an alleyway nearby, and store owners greeted their patrons loudly as they entered through the doors. Aahna nodded at a few of them as she walked by. The air never smelled like any one thing. She could walk by one store and take in the fried oil used for battered snacks. A moment later, the sweet smell of rosewater could fill her nostrils as deserts were handed to impatient customers.

The evening had brought about cooler temperatures, and Aahna wrapped her sari around her for warmth. She hadn't changed from her open foot slippers to her covered shoes yet, and now her feet were taking the brunt of the coolness. It was early February and the weather had finally adjusted to its more seasonal pattern.

As Aahna turned into the alleyway that led to her house, she noticed her brother's rickshaw out in front. I guess he finished early, Aahna thought to herself. At the same moment, she heard shouting coming from the house next door.

"I told you...you...to come home straight after...w-work!" The voice bellowed, and Aahna recognized the drunken slurs of her neighbor, Vikas, almost immediately.

Aahna stood quietly outside for a moment. Her mother had told her many times not to interfere, but Raina, her friend and no doubt the unwilling participant on the other side of this argument, sounded like she needed help. She couldn't hear anything for a few seconds, and then there was a loud crash of what sounded like pots and pans clanging to the floor. Aahna held her breath. Should she go in? Should she get Sourav? As if on cue, Sourav opened the door to their house and came outside.

"What are you lurking out here for?" he said to his sister. "You should come inside now."

"I think we should go in there and help her!" Aahna pleaded.

"You know how it goes. Even if we go in there now, he'll do the same thing tomorrow. He's a drunk." Sourav pulled on Aahna's arm to bring her inside.

"We can't just do nothing. She's my friend!" Aahna stated angrily.

"Keep your voice down! Do you really want him to come out here and hear us talking about him?"

"Let him!" Aahna glared at the house where her friend lived.

"Talk to her tomorrow, and ask her what she wants us to do. She'll say the same thing, trust me. Now come inside."

Aahna reluctantly followed Sourav inside. She could have sworn she heard the faint murmuring of crying as she walked away from Raina's house.

The houses on their strip were all identical. They each had two rooms only, and a small area for a few hot plates. The residents all shared one outhouse style bathroom further down the way, and the water pump was located in the same area. Sourav ducked his head in the doorway and Aahna followed suit. Their mother, Ruma, was squatting by the hot plates, boiling some rice and cutting up a few vegetables.

"Hi, Ma," Aahna said as she dropped her bag onto the floor and kicked off her shoes. She threw herself onto the small cot and rested there for a minute. "You're home early," she continued to her brother.

"Business wasn't that good today. It seems like more and more people are buying cars now. It makes no sense, since there's no room for these cars on the roads. How about they build better roads first and then we can start introducing all these other modes of transportation?"

Aahna rolled her eyes. Her brother loved ranting. She turned her attention to her mother.

"Ma, why can't Raina just leave Vikas?"

"Don't be silly. Life doesn't work that way. You can't just get up and leave whenever you want to."

"But he's a drunk!" Aahna protested. "Why should she have to deal with all that? They don't even have children yet."

"Her parents would never let her come back. It's her destiny to be with this man."

"This is insane! How can that be your answer to everything?"

Ruma raised her left eyebrow at her daughter. "You know this is how life is. Stop watching those movies and thinking that some hero is going to come and rescue you from this world. It won't happen."

"It could happen!" Aahna said without thinking.

Ruma looked at Aahna quizzically.

"I just mean, am I really destined to marry some drunk and spend the rest of my life working and getting beaten by him?" Aahna stood up angrily. "What is the point of me living then?"

"Stop being so dramatic," Sourav jumped in. "Ma and I will do whatever it takes to find you a good man, preferably someone who is allergic to alcohol." He winked at his sister.

"Baba was a good man," Aahna said quietly, thinking fondly of her father.

"Let us change this topic," Ruma announced. "Dear, how was work today?"

"It was fine," Aahna said, sitting back down on the cot. "Everyone there is quite nice."

"It was really nice of Sunil Sir to fix you up with this afternoon job. He was always such a good boy."

"He still is. His wife is a different matter though."

Ruma laughed. "Well, she came from a good family, which is all his parents were looking for."

"That doesn't mean everything you know."

"I know, but it helps."

Aahna sighed. This conversation was going nowhere. "I'm going to go for a walk if you don't mind. I'll be back before dinner."

"Take a shawl before you go. It's chilly outside now." Ruma turned back to her cooking.

Aahna glanced at her family as she stepped out of her house. She could tell they were content with their lives, although content and resigned could sometimes be mistaken for the same thing.

Aahna threw the shawl around her shoulders as she stepped into the cool night air. Dogs barked and jumped around her crazily. She ignored them and walked on the other side of the road. This time of evening was the only time she felt any peace. Most people had gone inside their houses at this point and were starting dinner. The streets weren't deserted, but relative to the rest of the day, they were definitely quieter. Aahna walked with her head down and started thinking of her father again. It had been bad luck that he passed away from a heart attack when she was only fifteen years old. But everything she remembered about him was still well pronounced. He was a kind man, always looking out for his youngest child. He was different than most of the other fathers who lived in her neighborhood. They were the very definition of the alpha-male. But Sujoy Roy was far more sensitive. He had always wanted Aahna to break away from this life, but he was helpless in getting her there. She loved him dearly for trying.

Her eyes started to well up as the memories came flooding back. She brushed them aside quickly, before anyone else could notice. In thinking of good men, her thoughts wandered to Daniel. There had only been two encounters, but for some reason, they were both deeply embedded in her mind. She had no idea what kind of man he was based on those two meetings. But she saw something in his eyes. Gentleness and a kindness that she hadn't seen in the men that were generally in her presence.

There were really only two types of men in her life, aside from the ones in her own family. The men who chose to ignore her, and the men who she wished would ignore her but instead lingered too long. She knew that was partially why her mother wanted to marry her off. After twenty-five years, Aahna needed to be claimed simply to be rid of all the snide looks.

Daniel had looked at her differently. Mainly he looked at her like a real person and treated her as such. Anyway, what did it matter? Daniel would be leaving in a few months and all of this would become moot. He probably already had a girlfriend.

Aahna shook her head. Why was she even thinking like this? He was just a foreigner that had been nice to the cleaning staff. Her own mundane life was causing her to read into this too much.

Aahna made her way out of the residential area onto the main road. She needed the distraction of the honking cars and people milling around everywhere, anything to get her mind off her current train of thought. She stopped by a nearby convenience store to purchase a small candy bar, even though it was nearly dinnertime. Walking into the store reminded her of the recently broken engagement with another store clerk. The locals still looked at Aahna with pity.
She knew it was only a matter of time before her mother and brother would find her someone new to marry. She cringed at the thought of it.

What if he turned out to be like Vikas? She imagined herself stronger than Raina. And her family more understanding if she had to walk away from someone like him. But what if she couldn't? What if she was required to accept her fate and spend her life with a wicked man that treated her badly? Her mother was a huge believer of fate and destiny. The majority of people in her country were. Sujoy Roy had thought otherwise and had tried to teach his daughter differently. Her fate was in no one else's hands but her own, he had always said.

Aahna turned the corner back onto her street and saw Raina near the water pump. She hurried over to her. "Are you okay?" she blurted out.

Raina looked up at her and smiled. Her eyes were swollen, and her left cheek was red, as if waiting for a bruise to appear shortly. "I'm okay," she whispered back.

"Oh Raina," Aahna said, looking at her face. "I'm so sorry."

"It's okay. He doesn't mean it. I was late today, and I shouldn't have been."

"This wasn't your fault. Why would you defend him?"

"You don't know him."

"I know him well enough."

Raina finished pumping her bucket of water and stood up straight. "You live in a fantasy world Aahna. A place where everyone is nice all the time. People get angry. Things happen."

"You can surround yourself with people who are nice," Aahna replied back.

"You'll grow up one day, and find out what life is really like. It's about responsibility and duty. If I have to be reminded on occasion of what my duty is, then so be it."

Aahna looked at her friend with mixed emotions. Part of her was sad for Raina, the other part was angry. Angry at Vikas for being a drunk; at Raina for accepting it; at her mother for thinking it was normal; at Sourav for being complacent. And at herself, for always talking about fate, but never actually challenging it.

Chapter Four

"I knew our paths would cross again one day." Daniel smiled as he opened the stairwell doors for Aahna.

Another day of work had passed and Aahna found herself leaving at the same time as her handsome acquaintance. She was surprised how much she looked forward to the possibility of seeing him, even if just briefly.

"I guess it was only a matter of time," Aahna replied back. "Why are you taking the stairs?"

"Exercise. I haven't had a chance to hit the gym since I've gotten here. Every time I go back to the hotel I end up just doing more work, or being so drained from the heat that I fall asleep early."

"That does not sound like a very glamorous life you are leading."

"Ha! Not in the least. It's been both routine, and well a little boring."

Aahna walked slowly in front of Daniel, making sure to look straight and not do anything clumsy, like fall down a step.

"Boring? I would have thought Sunil Sir would have shown you the sites by now." Aahna was careful not to brush too closely to Daniel as they turned the corner on the landing. She noticed Daniel retained a safe distance from her as well.

"He promised he would, as have a couple of the other guys in the office. They've taken me out to a few different restaurants, but no one seems too eager to wander around town with me."

"That is unfortunate. There is plenty to see and do in this city."

"I know! Everyone back home keeps asking me about India and I have no details to share, except about the room service and the inside lobby of this building. I wish I could just go exploring one day."

Aahna noticed Daniel glancing at her as they made their way down another flight of stairs.

He cleared his throat. "Perhaps, you could show me one day."

Aahna almost tripped on the next step.

"Sir?"

"You live here and you seem to have a lot to say. I think you would make a fine guide."

Aahna was finding it hard to concentrate on both walking and stopping her heart from beating out of its chest.

"Sir, I don't think that's wise."

"Listen, I understand that you and I aren't supposed to be friends. I don't know if I fully agree with it, but I'm guessing I should somewhat respect it." Daniel paused on the next landing. "But I haven't made any actual friends here. And for whatever reason, I find it really easy to talk to you."

Aahna stopped as well on the top stair of the next flight and glanced up at Daniel. He was wearing what seemed to be a shy smile, which was surprising to her since he always appeared so confident.

"That is nice of you to say, Sir." Aahna hesitated. "But I still do not think any of this is appropriate. There are rules for this kind of thing."

"And what kind of thing might this be?" Daniel's voice started to rise.

"We cannot be friends, we cannot be anything."

"I can only imagine that you have spent your entire life being told what you can and can't do. Why are you so willing to accept it?"

"And why must you not accept it?" Aahna's volume began to match Daniel's. "Is it because you are so used to always getting what you want?"

Daniel seemed surprised at Aahna's retort.

She, herself was surprised.

"I don't think that it's right the way they treat you here," Daniel said quietly.

"It isn't your place to solve a two thousand year old caste problem."

Daniel didn't respond. Instead he made his way from the landing and continued down the stairs quickly. When he passed Aahna, he didn't glance at her, and kept walking.

Aahna hurried after him down the stairs. "Sir?" she called. "Sir, I should not have been so abrupt." She had no idea why she was treating him with such an indifferent attitude.

"It doesn't matter, I got the point."

"No, please just hear me out," Aahna protested. Was this it? This was how their fleeting relationship was going to end? These thoughts tumbled through her head as the edge of her shoe got caught on the subsequent step. She gasped as her body flew forward and her bag went flying out of her hand. She flailed her arms wildly trying to grasp the banister on one side, the wall on the other, anything. It took only a second for Daniel to turn around and raise his arms up. He grabbed her at her waist, falling back two steps in the process. Aahna's body flew into him and he held onto her tight.

His right arm reached for the banister for support and the two stood on the stairs in a prolonged embraced. Aahna's breathing was heavy against his chest. She could smell the cologne again. Aahna felt him pull away slightly as he looked down at her.

"Are you okay?"

He was still holding onto her with one arm wrapped around her thin waist. It was the one part not covered by the sari, and his skin on her skin left her feeling warm and caused her face to turn a slight shade of red.

She nodded, and then realizing the situation, pulled out of his embrace. "Thank you, Sir. I don't know what came over me."

"You were running pretty fast." Daniel smiled at her now, as if their prior conversation was forgotten. He stepped toward the landing and grabbed her bag which lay there, its contents strewn on the floor. He started to pick them up one by one.

Aahna hurried forward again, this time more carefully. "You don't have to do that, I can manage." She squatted down and grabbed the bag from him.

"At least let me help you," Daniel said. He reached for her pen the same time she did. Their hands grazed for a moment and a spark ignited from the edge of Aahna's fingertip straight to her heart. She looked up at him solemnly. He had returned to picking up other items from the floor and appeared to no longer be paying attention to her.

When they were done, Aahna hoisted the bag upon her shoulder and they both started to walk down the remaining flight of stairs, this time together and slower.

"It's funny. All the women I know carry three different kinds of makeup, mirrors, creams and gum in their purse. I guess you're not like most women huh?"

"I am like a lot of women in this country."

"Oh right," Daniel said.

Aahna cringed. Did she always have to be so flippant? Daniel was one of the few men in her life that spoke to her politely and treated her with respect. Her mind wandered to Rana, and her demon of a husband. Suddenly her father's words about fate came back to her.

"I will take you around the city." The words came out of her mouth before she even had a chance to process what she was saying. She saw Daniel's face light up.

"Are you sure? I mean, I completely understand why you are hesitant."

Aahna nodded. "I am sure," she said, even though it wasn't remotely true. She looked at him and smiled reassuringly.

His eyes crinkled as he smiled back and Aahna's sudden courage was replaced by the weakness in her knees.

The pair reached the final landing and Daniel leaned past her to open the exit door. The sunlight burst in and shone on both their faces. In one instant, their quiet oasis was disrupted with the noises of the cars and people that awaited them on the other side of the door. Daniel must have felt the same way because he slammed the door shut and threw his body against it. The sunlight disappeared along with the commotion.

The two stood still, the only sound that resonated was their quiet, patterned breathing.

"I see you are still not used to this?" Aahna said smiling.

"Can anyone ever get used to all of this?"

"Over time you will start to see the positive aspects of this city."

"Well that will be your duty this weekend. Make me fall in love..."

Aahna's heart skipped a beat.

"...with your city," Daniel finished.

Aahna barely heard the last part.

***

It was eight-thirty in the morning when Daniel's alarm rang. Slamming on the snooze button, he rolled over and buried his face in the pillow. It was Saturday, and he was finally able to sleep in for a little while longer. The jet lag had subsided a few weeks earlier, but the heat and the noise and the congestion were getting to him. He still had over four months left in India, but in his current state, he couldn't imagine actually getting used to any of the surroundings. The term culture shock was an understatement; his system was more in awe of its new habitat. Sunil had mentioned that Daniel was actually quite lucky the hotel location was on the outskirts of the city, where the noise pollution wasn't so prevalent. In Sunil's apartment, they were woken by six in the morning to the sounds of merchants selling rice, crows asserting their dominance, and of course the symphony of horns coming from cars, trucks, and rickshaws alike.

Daniel buried his head into his pillow further, enjoying the coziness of his modern hotel room. The alarm rang again, the ten minute snooze expiring. He slammed his hand down on it for a second time, and finally lifted his head and body to a seated position. His rubbed his eyes, gave a large yawn and leaned back against the headboard.

Today was the day he was meeting Aahna for his unofficial tour of the city, a notion that left him feeling excited and uneasy at the same time. He still didn't quite know what to think of her. She seemed reserved initially when they met, but had since opened up in an almost precocious way. He remembered when they first met, how Aahna could barely look at him, and now when they saw each other, her eyes barely left his. Since the stairwell incident they had run into each other almost every day. There was a somewhat strange anticipation of their proposed date, and Daniel, who had originally suggested it as a friendly gesture was now feeling nervous about the potential outcome.

He was attracted to Aahna, he knew that much. He was surprised at how often he would make sure to go into the kitchen at a certain time to run into her intentionally. And in an immature way, he would make sure that Sunil was never around. Daniel hadn't pulled stunts like that since he was in high school when he was trying to hide girls from his parents. All of it was an adrenaline rush, and he couldn't be certain if this was just a spiteful way of getting back at a society that told him he couldn't befriend someone. Regardless, he was delightfully engrossed with Aahna's company and genuinely wanted to spend more time with her. He knew very little about Aahna, her life, her past, her family. Their conversations had been superficial at best, but he had a feeling there was a whole lot more. He hadn't met anyone like her before, and he was intrigued enough to defy Sunil's request.

Daniel didn't really believe that Aahna was going to fall for him in any serious fashion; she actually seemed to have another agenda for wanting to spend time with him. But he didn't really care. He was lonely in this city of millions and any non-work companionship was a welcome change.

The phone rang, the hotel concierge reminding Daniel that the car he had requested would be arriving in thirty minutes. He quickly got out of bed, showered and changed, and then headed downstairs to grab some breakfast.

Aahna had asked Daniel to meet him at their first stop on the city tour, Victoria Memorial.

"Will my driver know where it is?" Daniel had asked her.

"If he doesn't, you better get a new driver," Aahna had responded back.

Daniel, like all people of his generation was tempted to look up the landmark on the internet and learn everything about it prior to actually viewing it. But he stopped himself, and realized he wanted to hear about it for the first time from Aahna.

When he arrived at their destination a short while later, he looked for Aahna through the car window. He saw her waiting near a stand selling coconut water in front of the main gates. At first glance, he almost didn't recognize her. Instead of the plain, cotton sari she donned for work, Aahna was wearing another traditional Indian outfit Daniel had seen his female staff wearing, a long top with fitted pants. Her hair, which was normally pulled back in a bun, was undone today, falling loosely around her shoulders. She appeared nervous as well and her eyes were darting back and forth, as if worried someone would see her.

Daniel still wasn't sure what had caused Aahna's change of heart in meeting him today, but he pushed the thought out of his mind as he got out of the car and headed in her direction.

Her face lit up when he came into her view, and the smile was disarming. No one had looked at Daniel like that in quite a long time, and he found himself quickening his step to meet her.

When they were finally face to face with each other, Daniel found he had no words. Aahna apparently had the same problem, so a silence sat between them.

The man selling the coconut water behind the stand suddenly yelled out something indecipherable. Daniel turned around and saw the man waving a large coconut shell with its top cut off and a straw struck through it.

"You should have some, if you haven't tried one yet," Aahna spoke up.

"I've seen those around everywhere. I'm actually allergic to coconuts." Daniel ignored the strange look Aahna gave him.

She spoke to the man waving the coconut in their native tongue and he nodded.

"Your people are allergic to a lot of things, no?"

"My people?"

"I mean, people from your part of the world? We've seen on the television all these things about being allergic."

"No one's allergic to anything here?"

"It's not as common."

"Well, studies say that allergies are part hereditary and part a product of the environment you grow up in," Daniel said. "So I guess it's possible that we have more allergies than people here. It would appear your immune system is naturally stronger than ours anyway."

"That is definitely the case," Aahna said. "Anyway, you are here now and you have avoided eating coconut, so how about we get started with our day?"

"I'm all yours," Daniel smiled, raising his arms.

Aahna's face turned a deep shade of red, as if he had said something inappropriate. Daniel realized he had made her feel uncomfortable with his casual forwardness.

"What's the name of the outfit you're wearing?" Daniel said, attempting to reduce any awkwardness. "Someone told me once but I've forgotten."

"It is called a *salwar kameez*. It is a common type of clothing that you can wear either very casually, or you can buy extremely fancy ones that girls wear at weddings."

Daniel couldn't come up with any more small talk that was even remotely interesting so he simply nodded. "Shall we go in?"

The two walked side by side through the main gates. The illustrious white structure stood in front of them in all of its glory. Daniel had been so focused on seeing Aahna he hadn't even noticed the magnificence of the building. They stood just inside of the gates to take in the full view of the large domed rooftop in the center, the garden that surrounded it, and the large archway that represented the main entryway.

"This is amazing," Daniel said. "I can't believe I've been here for nearly two months and have yet to see this."

"It is definitely the most famous landmark here in Kolkata," Aahna said. "Come on, let's go inside."

They headed through the main entrance together, Daniel paying the foreigner price for his ticket, and the local price for Aahna's ticket.

"So tell me about this place," Daniel said, handing Aahna her admission ticket.

For the next hour, Daniel listened patiently as his tour guide explained the ins and outs of Victoria Memorial. She explained how it was designed by the British as a memorial to the late Queen Victoria and proudly mentioned that the entire proceeds for the cost of construction were donated by Kolkata's inhabitants. He watched her discuss the Calcutta Gallery, explaining the history of her beloved city from Job Charnok (traditionally known as the British founder of Kolkata) to the time when Kolkata was no longer the once prominent capital city of India.

They headed into the Royal Gallery where Daniel stopped to admire the paintings of various British royalties, including Queen Victoria herself. He was most fascinated with the artistry of the Indian landscapes, created coincidentally, by the Daniells, an uncle and nephew team from England. And his thirst for knowledge was quenched as they headed into the library to view books dating back to 1870, including plays written by none other than Shakespeare himself.

Their final stop was the garden. Daniel rested against the upper balcony to appreciate the full view of its beauty, while Aahna made her way around the perimeter. He watched her for a few minutes, as she walked with her hands behind her back. She seemed peaceful and calm, even if just for a moment. The sun reflected against the back of the building, and subsequently engulfed the entire garden, including Aahna. Daniel stood quietly on the balcony, and watched as the light shone on her face. Even at this distance, he could still make out the details of her milk chocolate complexion, her large, expressive eyes and the smile that was still on her face. He couldn't stop himself from staring just at her, even as she stood amongst a gorgeous shrine of green landscapes and bronze statues. He was having a great time, the first in a long time. Everything seemed simple, even despite the initial reservations about the day, and he knew that had a lot to do with Aahna.

After a few more minutes of gazing, Daniel headed down the marble stairs and joined her in the garden.

"This is overly impressive I must say," Daniel said as he met up with his companion.

"I told you this city had a lot to offer."

"This city isn't the only thing." Daniel decided to test the waters. He had promised himself he would be cognizant of her society's rules, but he wasn't staying in India forever, and his confidence was now overriding his general sensibility.

Aahna didn't respond to his comment. "We should go," she said as she herded him out of the main gates. They walked in silence the rest of the way.

When they reached the coconut stand again, Aahna spoke. "Are you ready for the next stop on our tour?"

"Actually hold on a second, did you want to sit on the bench out here for a little bit?" Daniel said.

Aahna glanced over at the bench and shook her head. "I would rather not."

"Why?"

"Inside, I believe most people thought I was a hired guide for you. If I was sitting on the bench and chatting they would think otherwise."

"I thought the fact that you're here with me today implies you actually don't care what people think."

"That's not entirely true," Aahna said.

Daniel sighed. He was wondering if they were ever going to be able to speak openly and honestly. "Why are you here?" he finally asked.

"I'm sorry?"

"Why did you agree to meet me? Every moment you remind me in some way that we can't be friends."

Aahna slowly sat down on the bench, the one that she was so hesitant to sit on just moments ago. She appeared defeated for some reason, as if she was trying to avoid this conversation at all costs.

Daniel remained standing near her and kept quiet. He didn't want her to shut down all together.

"You are right," Aahna said. "I am sorry for being so up and down with everything. It is just that I have never done anything like this before. I am not exactly sure how I am supposed to act."

Daniel hesitated, but finally decided to sit down on the bench anyway. He kept his distance, and didn't look at her, but merely focused his gaze in front of him at the traffic congestion and tourists milling in and out of the gates. He watched as a small boy played with a balloon in front of them, and as several young men started a cricket match at the large park across the street.

Daniel took a deep breath.

"What do you think this is exactly?" he started. Hearing no response, he looked over at Aahna.

She kept her eyes on her shoes. Her fingers were grasping the edge of the bench seat and he could sense the tension up her spine.

"Aahna?" he whispered softly.

"I am just your tour guide," she said quietly.

Daniel leaned back in his seat. "If that were true, you wouldn't be so anxious around me. I saw the way you kept looking at all the other locals inside. You thought they were looking at us, but they weren't. So I'm going to ask you again, what do you think this is exactly?"

"What is your intention?" Aahna replied back.

Daniel paused. This was the second time in only a few days that someone had asked him this question, he thought, remembering Sunil and Moumita's confrontation earlier.

"Well," he started. "I actually haven't thought that far ahead. I like you Aahna. And where I come from, when you like someone, you spend time with them. That's all."

"Why do you like me?" she now locked directly at him. "I mean, why *me*?"

"I met *you* first," he joked.

Aahna's face was blank.

Daniel continued again. "I really don't have an answer, at least one that can make you happy. I find myself thinking about you. A lot. And I don't know why. These things just happen I guess."

"I don't know what to say."

"It's true. I don't know what it means, and I don't know what will come of it. But that's how I feel right now." Daniel hadn't had a conversation like this in a long time, and even then, it wasn't as seemingly forced. With other girls he dated, the physical aspect of the relationship had been reached by this point and therefore the feelings were generally understood. Everything was different with Aahna. They were barely allowed to sit on a bench together so he had no choice but to recite out his thoughts.

Out of the corner of his eye, he thought he saw Aahna's lips curl up into a smile. She got up from the bench slowly and walked a couple of steps forward. Then she turned around to look at him, and her smile turned into a full grin.

"Come on Daniel, we don't want to be late for the next stop."

Daniel smiled back, realizing her voice had never sounded sweeter, then when he finally heard the sound of his own name.

***

It was nearly six in the evening when Daniel and Aahna had finished their tour. The sun was slowly beginning its descent and streetlamps were turning on everywhere. The weather was still relatively mild, and the evening brought a welcome relief to the intense heat that had filled the day.

After Victoria Memorial, Daniel had been taken to the Birla Mandir - a famous Hindu temple – where they both had offered flowers to the many Hindu gods on display.

"Do you believe in all of these Gods?" Daniel had asked.

"I do, yes. They each represent something different. For example, Saraswati is the Goddess of Knowledge, whereas Ganesh is the Remover of Obstacles," Aahna explained. "Different Hindus from different parts of India may worship one God more over the other, but we believe they all provide something valuable."

After a quick lunch of soup and sandwiches at a nearby restaurant, they headed to the main amusement attraction, Nico Park. The site was swarming with young kids and their parents, as everyone was either waiting in lines for the rides, or standing around the various food kiosks nibbling on deep-fried anything. Daniel noticed people glancing at them as they entered, the same looks they got at the restaurant earlier. Even his driver, Mukesh, had glanced back in the rear-view mirror on more than one occasion. He ignored the looks, but kept an eye on Aahna to make sure she didn't notice. They were finally getting comfortable with each other and he didn't want anything to ruin that.

After their chat on the bench in the morning she had loosened up considerably. She laughed heartily at Daniel's jokes, kept up the appropriate amount of eye contact, and retained a close distance to him as they walked. In other words, she was turning into the perfect date. Daniel was trying to avoid thinking about how the evening would end, but alas it had almost arrived.

"This was the final stop on the tour," Aahna said as they headed back to the waiting car. "What did you think of the planetarium?"

"It was great," Daniel said, distracted by thoughts of his next move.

"I am glad you enjoyed it. And I hope you enjoyed the whole day. Thank you for asking me to be your guide. I had a lovely time."

"No, thank you Aahna. This day was better than I imagined it would be. And now at least I have something to tell my family back in Canada."

"I can take the bus back home now. Your car will take you back to the hotel."

"Have dinner with me," Daniel blurted out.

"I'm sorry?"

"Would you like to have dinner with me tonight? My treat. For being such a fantastic guide." Daniel tried not to appear desperate, but he wasn't sure when the next time Aahna would be out of her house like this.

"Okay," Aahna said slowly. "But then I really do have to head home after that."

"Of course. If you don't mind my asking, where does your family think you are right now?"

"With a friend from work. Which isn't a complete lie." Aahna winked at him.

They made their way to the car and piled into the backseat.

"Where should we go for dinner?" Daniel asked.

"There is a place near your office actually. It is called Bar-B-Q Land. There should not be too many people there today since it is mostly popular for the office crowd during the week."

"Sounds great. Mukesh, do you know where this place is?"

"I do, Sir," Mukesh answered back in a somewhat unfriendly tone. Daniel glanced at him through the rearview mirror. He was getting tired of the attitude from his usually pleasant driver.

"Can I talk to you for a second please?" Daniel said, getting out of the car.

Mukesh followed him while Aahna waited.

"Is there a problem here?" Daniel said when they were a safe distance away.

"Sir, it is not my place to say anything."

"Then it is also not your place to imply anything by your tone or your looks. I've noticed you watching us the entire day. I need to know if there is a problem."

"Sir, if you wanted a tour guide, I could have recommended many people. I have many friends in the business. *Male* friends. And if you wanted female companionship, well I can arrange that as well."

Daniel raised an eyebrow. "I know Aahna well. That's why I asked her to come with me today."

"Sir, I am guessing her family does not know she is with you. And I am guessing that if they found out, there would be a lot of trouble. This is not appropriate."

"Are you planning on telling her family?"

"No, of course not. I mean, I don't even know who she is. Wandering around town is one thing. But now dinner? Are you certain about this?"

Daniel looked over at the car, where Aahna sat in the backseat, fidgeting with her hair. A slight glow from a nearby streetlight shone into the car, and her face was caught in the radiance of it. She looked over at him in that moment and gave a small smile. He returned it, and then looked at Mukesh.

"I am certain Mukesh. And I would appreciate it if you kept your thoughts to yourself from now on." With that, Daniel turned and headed back to the car.

A short while later, the car pulled up in front of Bar-B-Q Land. True to Aahna's words, the restaurant was filled with only a handful of people, working the Saturday shift in one of the nearby offices. Rickshaws lined the front of the restaurant, and the drivers all stood around, laughing and chatting with each other.

"Sir, I will wait for you over there," Mukesh said, pointing to the end of the street where other cars were parked.

Daniel stepped out of the car, catching the eye of almost all the rickshaw drivers. Their banter slowed down as they watched him walk around to the other side and opened the door. Aahna stepped out and the banter ceased completely.

Aahna kept her head down as she walked into the restaurant. Daniel watched the rickshaw drivers watching her and then watching him. He rolled his eyes and headed into the restaurant.

After being seated, Aahna explained to Daniel how the food arrangements would work. Essentially staff would continuously bring out various meats, which the guests would then barbeque on the open grills in front of them.

"I hope you are hungry," she said. "There is a full buffet you are expected to eat after the meat course."

Daniel laughed. "I think we'll be here for a while then."

When the first round of tandoori spiced chicken came out, Daniel leaned back and watched as Aahna placed the items on the grill.

"Can I ask you something?" Aahna said, not looking at Daniel, but instead staring at the chicken as she rotated it on the grill. "How is a man like you not married yet?"

"You sound like my mother," Daniel said, chuckling.

"Is it too personal of a question?"

"No, I don't mind. I haven't found the right person yet. I'm only thirty-two actually. I've been focused more on getting my career going then looking for a wife."

"Surely you have had many girlfriends then."

"I wouldn't say many," Daniel said coyly. "I've had two serious relationships in my life. One, when I was in university and another that just ended last year."

"What happened with that one?"

Daniel hesitated. He wasn't sure if he wanted to bring up this part of his life.

Aahna must have noticed his hesitation because she quickly grabbed the chicken off the grill and placed it on his plate. "First course is ready," she said.

Daniel took a bite. "This is delicious," he said genuinely. As they ate in silence for a few minutes, Daniel scanned the restaurant to notice the other patrons. They were mostly young men, the kind that worked for him and Sunil back at TargetLife. They were laughing and joking around, interchanging English and Bengali in their conversations. A couple of them would occasionally look over at Daniel and Aahna, but for the most part they minded their own business.

Daniel knew that Aahna was out on a great limb accepting his offer to have dinner. There was no risk on his part to any of this. If he wanted her to open up to him, he was going to have to show his vulnerable side now.

"We dated for three years, and well, I broke her heart," Daniel said.

Aahna lifted her head up, a look of curiosity on her face.

Daniel took a deep breath. "We were inseparable, best friends. I adored her. Our relationship was almost too easy."

"What did you do?" Aahna asked, almost in a whisper.

"I used to have to travel regularly to the States for work. There was a girl that worked for the client in Boston. We became good friends."

Aahna leaned forward in her chair. Daniel realized she probably only heard these kinds of stories in the movies.

"Nothing happened," he assured her. "But it almost did. And I realized how easily I was willing to let my entire relationship go for nothing more than what would be short term pleasure."

"You said you did not do anything though?"

"It didn't matter. I felt awful for letting it get as far as it did. I came clean with my girlfriend, and in the process of trying to mend our relationship I ruined it completely."

"Why did you do it? I mean, why would you just not stay away from that girl in Boston?"

"It's hard to explain. We had this intense chemistry, which yes, in hindsight I should have avoided at all costs. But it's hard to control...some things." Daniel's voice tapered off.

Aahna leaned back in her chair, as if pondering everything Daniel had told her.

"Anyway, I realized after the break-up, that I couldn't be that guy anymore. The one that just did whatever he wanted without thinking of the consequences. That's why I've been so hesitant with you."

"I don't understand."

"You must know by now that I feel something for you, or that there is something between us. I can't explain why or how. I just think that it's worth exploring. But like I said, I don't want to do anything again without thinking through the consequences. I can't even imagine what this would mean for you, in your world."

Aahna remained quiet.

"Please say something," Daniel urged.

"I am...confused." Aahna started to speak again but was interrupted when the waiter came around with the next round of fish. He removed the chicken trays, poured water into their glasses, gave them a skeptical look and headed back into the kitchen.

"I should tell you that the real reason I agreed to join you today was because I was angry at my family."

Now it was Daniel's turn to look confused. "What does your family have to do with this?"

"They have my life laid out for me. What I will do in five years, ten years, who I will marry, everything. I wanted to do something that no one expected. Something that wasn't written out for me since the moment I was born." Aahna paused. "And therefore, something they can never take away from me."

"Are you using me?" Daniel asked. This conversation was not going where he had hoped. In fact, he was beginning to see how all the girls in his life must now feel. It was depressing and humiliating all at the same time.

"I think I am...trying you out." Aahna played with the fish on her plate, moving it around in circles but not actually eating any of it. "I really did have a lovely time with you. And I enjoy spending time with you as well. I would not have accepted your offer if I felt otherwise. But I am not simply here as some naïve girl who is smitten with a foreign man. I should be allowed to be here, in spite of everything."

"So you want me to help you prove some point to society?"

"Is that not why you are partially here? Because someone told you not to be? I know what the driver said to you. I have a feeling you see me as some sort of challenge."

The waiter came around again with more food and this time Daniel waved him off. He was no longer hungry and the sheer presence of a third person in this intense discussion was beginning to irritate him. He knew Aahna was right. He had his own intentions originally. But after this day, his feelings were different. They had evolved, he was certain of that. And he was angry that Aahna had seen right through him.

"Now what?" Daniel said, after some time.

"Well for one thing, I think the waiter assumes you do not know how you are supposed to eat here."

"And what do you think?"

"I think we both started this day with one frame of mind. But I believe we are leaving it with another."

Aahna leaned forward in her chair, and placed her hand on the table. "If I want to start really living my life, then I have to start living."

Daniel reached out his hand and gestured towards hers. "Can I...?" he trailed off.

"Not unless you want a picture to be taken and posted somewhere." Aahna placed her hand back under the table. "But know that for the rest of the night, I would be hoping that you could."

Chapter Five

The dirt crunched under Aahna's shoe as she made her way from the bus stop to her home. It was windier than normal and the shawl Aahna usually kept in her bag was wrapped tightly around her petite figure. Flags and tin store signs were whipping about furiously all around her. Store owners were pulling their merchandise from the front of the store and mothers were holding on tight to their children. Aahna zigzagged her way through everyone, keeping her head down and charging forward. Raina had invited her over for tea and she didn't want to be late. It was one of the few nights her husband wasn't home; therefore a simple invitation for tea naturally became a special event.

Aahna hurried past the rickshaws lined up at the end of the block, ignored the drivers whistling at her, walked by the other houses on the street including her own, and promptly knocked on Raina's door.

The door swung open, more aggressive than usual due to the heavy wind. Raina reached her arm out and pulled Aahna into the house before anything could fly by them.

Aahna removed her shawl and patted down her hair as Raina headed over to the stove to start boiling the water.

"Pleasant outside?" Raina said.

"You could say that," Aahna answered.

"At least it's not cold wind."

"Wind is wind, nothing good comes from it." Aahna pulled up a small chair from the corner and joined Raina near the stove.

"Where is Vikas tonight?"

"Working the late shift at the pharmaceutical store. Their regular employee is sick today or something."

"How have things been with Vikas?" Aahna asked, diplomatically.

"The same," Raina said. "He really wants us to have a child now."

"What?" Aahna asked aghast, forgetting about diplomacy. "You want to bring a child into this kind of environment?"

"I was brought into one," Raina answered nonchalantly, as she poured out the water into two awaiting teacups. She placed in the tealeaves, steeping it with a small strainer, stirred in the milk and sugar, and handed one of the cups to her friend.

"Do you think he'll stop after having a child?"

"Drinking? I don't think so. One doesn't have anything to do with the other."

"I suppose not," Aahna said, not sure what to say next.

"Enough of this. Tell me how is Sunil Da, and how is the office job is going."

"Sunil Da is fine. I run into him most days and we chat briefly. I'm not sure how much his wife is alright with us seeing each other twice a day now."

"I don't understand what her problem is with you," Raina said, taking a sip of tea.

"She thinks we should all be ignored, barely spoken to, and certainly not befriended."

"She married the wrong man."

"I think he married the wrong woman," Aahna said and they both started laughing.

Outside the wind continued howling. The walls of the small, fragile house shook slightly and the pots on the stove teetered precariously. Raina reached over to settle them.

Aahna watched her friend as she maneuvered around the area, placing fragile items on lower shelves and securing the windows. They had been friends all of two years, since Raina had married Vikas and moved into the house that was neighboring Aahna's. It was actually Aahna and Vikas that had grown up together and he stayed in the small house even after his parents had passed on. At first, Vikas had kept Raina in the house at all times, not sure how to handle a new wife. But when Raina started working as the maid for a nearby restaurant, Aahna would run into her in the streets and the two had begun chatting. They became fast friends, and it was nice for Aahna to finally be able to confide in someone that hadn't known her and her family since she was a child. But Aahna wondered now if she could trust her with the latest news in her life, that of the budding relationship with a white man. She knew she had no choice in the matter. Aahna was bursting to tell someone and there was no one else she could think of.   "Raina, can you sit down for a second?"

"Of course. Is everything all right?"

"I need to tell you something, but you need to promise me that you won't tell anyone."

"I promise. Aahna, what is it?"

Aahna took a deep breath. She wasn't even sure where to begin. Her thoughts were all jumbled and it took her a few moments to cohesively string them together. She looked at her friend, and then plunged into the story, starting from the moment she first met Daniel.

Raina's eyes widened as the story unfolded, as Aahna spoke about the mutual attraction, the stairwell discussion, and then finally, their trip around Kolkata. She ended the tale with the conversation she and Daniel had shared. Where their true feelings had been translated into words and where Aahna's once still heart had finally begun to beat.

Raina remained silent when Aahna had finished speaking. She looked around the room, as if trying to eschew what she had just heard. "So," Raina started. "Do you...I mean, does he...what I'm trying to say is...what happens now?"

"I don't actually know. It's only been a few days since we spoke. I've run into him briefly at the office, but we haven't been able to chat about anything."

"Are you going to marry him?" Raina asked, incredulously.

"I don't think...that's possible," Aahna said slowly.

"Okay good. So this is just some kind of rite of passage before your mother marries you off?"

"I don't know how to explain what it is. When I first met him, I thought about him sometimes. But now that I know he feels the same way, I think about him always."

"Always?"

"I've never felt like this before. His face is always in the back of mind. I replay conversations that we've had and I go over and over the moments when he looks at me."

"Is it possible you're just caught up in the notion that a foreign man is actually pursuing you? Or even the fact that your family constantly brings up marriage and this is your way of rebelling. Effective, I might add."

"I thought about that. But then I realized I can't control how I feel. I wish I could. Wouldn't life be simpler that way?" Aahna paused and stared out the window. "I am happy on the days when he smiles at me, and I die on the days when he doesn't."

"You can't do this. If anyone were to find out..."

"No one will find out. That's why you have to promise not to tell anyone."

"What is the goal though? He's going to leave for Canada and you will be left here with a broken heart. Did you think of that?"

"Every day. I think of that every day."

"Do you believe he's going to ask you to go back with him?"

"I don't know!" Aahna protested. "We haven't thought through anything. I just wanted to tell someone. I wanted my good friend to know how happy I am. In this moment, at this time. Regardless of what happens three months from now or three days from now, I am never going to feel this way again. Can't I just enjoy it?" She stood up and started pacing around the house.

Raina watched her for a little while. "I don't want to see you get hurt."

"I can't say what path my life is going to take. Who I will marry and what kind of man he will be. But at least I get to have this right now. I need to believe, that in my entire life, I deserve this one moment of happiness. Is that so wrong?"

"No, of course it isn't. I want you to be happy enough for the both of us."

Aahna looked at her friend and smiled wistfully. Everything she was saying was something Raina was never going to experience. She was trapped in her world and there was very little she felt empowered to do.

Aahna kneeled down in front of Raina and clasped both of her hands. She looked up at her friend. "I wish that I could take away your pain. I wish that every day."

"I know you do."

"I want you to have hope. Hope that something good can come into your life, when you least expect it."

Raina smiled at Aahna. "You should go. Go and live the life we both know you deserve."

Aahna got up and grabbed her shawl. "I'll talk to you later," she said, as she opened the door and headed out to face the bitter wind.

***

Eight days, twenty-two hours, and thirteen minutes. Aahna aggressively dusted the desktops in the office as she counted how long it had been since she had last seen Daniel. At that time, he had briefly mentioned his numerous meetings throughout the city which would take him out of the office most afternoons. The previous weekend had been occupied when Sunil had suddenly decided to invite Daniel on a family trip to Delhi for three days. All of this had resulted in minimal interaction and maximum longing. Daniel had profusely apologized, but to no avail. It was of no use to finally have someone profess their feelings only to have that person seemingly abandon ship and continue living life as if nothing had changed.

Aahna knew it wasn't Daniel's fault. His work priorities came first, after all, that was the reason why he was in her country to begin with. But after not having any proper conversations following their monumental dinner, Aahna was beginning to feel slighted, and almost embarrassed. She had practically gushed about her situation to Raina, when in actuality, the new couple (could that term even be used yet?) had spent more time defining their relationship than experiencing it. Not that she had any idea how to experience it. She was hoping Daniel would take the lead on next steps. Would there be another meal involved? A movie, perhaps? And at what point would the relationship go from simply talking and laughing to something more? Something that made Aahna feel embarrassed all over again.

She hesitated to think that Daniel's plan was to simply keep
her around while he was available in Kolkata, and disregard all notions
of her as soon as he stepped on the plane. She didn't want to foresee
that far in the future. Besides, Aahna felt she could sense the kindness
in Daniel's heart. That everything he had uttered that day was genuine.
Now if only she could be in his presence again.

Aahna peered over at his desk in the corner. His chair was
tucked in neatly and the desk lamp was turned off. He had either left
for the day already or was at one of his offsite meetings. Sunil's office
light was also turned off, which meant the pair were most likely
somewhere together. Aahna felt a pang of jealousy for the amount of
time Sunil was able to spend with Daniel. She even felt jealous when
she had heard about the Delhi trip. Why should Moumita be allowed to
spend more time with Daniel than anything she had yet to achieve?
Aahna wasn't normally a jealous person, but then again, she had never
had such strong feelings for someone. She was beginning to realize why
there was generally as much good as there was bad in new
relationships.

There was that word again. Relationship. She hit herself on the
head lightly to get the thought out of her mind. Just as she was about
to get herself all riled up on her perpetual naïveté, the front glass doors
to the office swung open and in walked the man on her mind.

His laptop bag was slung casually over his shoulder, his half-
sleeved collared shirt was tucked neatly into his khaki pants (Daniel had
once mentioned it was called a golf shirt, but Aahna still didn't get it),
and his brown belt matched his brown casual shoes. He walked towards
her with a smile on his face and ran a hand through the wavy, blond
hair that covered his head. For a second, Aahna actually thought he
was walking in slow motion and had to blink twice to re-focus her gaze
into reality.

"You're still here!" Daniel proclaimed.

"I am almost done my shift," Aahna said. She tried to sound nonchalant, as if she wasn't waiting around by the desks with the hope that Daniel might return.

"Good, I'm glad. We haven't gotten a chance to talk. Everything has been so hectic the last couple of weeks."

"I hadn't noticed," Aahna said. Was that taking it too far? She tried to tone down the casualness in her voice. "How have you been?" she asked, a little more politely.

"Tired, stressed, the usual. We've been trying to get some new graphic designers on board but we haven't had too much luck. A lot of people seem to think that working for a company whose headquarters are in North America is a betrayal of their Indian values. But this is a global economy people! We all need to collaborate!" Daniel raised his arms in the air with a sense of exasperation.

Aahna squinted her eyes. "Maybe if you explained to them how their work would increase jobs here in India, and also how they could later use their connections and skills in their own career path, they would be more willing to join forces with you."

"I've tried that," Daniel sighed. "And so has Sunil. This company needs another spokesperson it would seem."

Aahna shrugged. This wasn't exactly the conversation she was hoping to have after seeing Daniel properly for the first time in as many days. Not that she expected Daniel to swoop in and lift her off her feet in a giant embrace. She paused for a second, actually visualizing a moment like that.

"Are you hungry?" Daniel interrupted her illusionary thoughts. He placed his laptop bag down and sat on the edge of the desk that Aahna had been dusting. Since it was late in the day, there were free to openly communicate without fear of someone still being in the office.

"My mother would expect me home after the shift," Aahna said.

"You could call her no? Tell her that you'll be late?"

"It is not that simple. I have no reason to be late."

"Oh, I see."

"We should make plans for another day. A day where I can come up with a story ahead of time?" Aahna didn't want Daniel to feel discouraged in what would no doubt be a far different situation than he was normally used to.

"Sure," Daniel said slowly. "How about on Thursday then? After your shift. We can grab dinner, or take a walk or something?"

"Yes, that sounds fine," Aahna smiled to show her genuine appreciation that things were evolving.

"If you're done your shift now, let me walk you to the bus stop."

"Okay, I just need about fifteen minutes."

"Take your time. I'll meet you in front of the stairwell."

Aahna blushed and Daniel smiled, as if he too was recollecting the last time they were in the stairwell.

The air was crisp as Aahna and Daniel headed out into the early evening. The area was relatively quiet as the evening shift of call-center employees had already started, and the daytime employees had all but gone home. A few stragglers lurked around but no one paid much attention to the foreigner and his not-so-foreign walking mate.

"Did I tell you my brother and his girlfriend are visiting here in two weeks?" Daniel started.

"You mean they are travelling together without being married?" Aahna inquired.

Daniel raised his eyebrow. "That wasn't the response I was expecting, but since you asked. Yes, they are travelling here together without being married. Well actually, he finally proposed to her. So technically she's his fiancée, but yeah, they aren't married yet."

"And her parents do not mind?"

"Mind what?" Daniel seemed to have trouble following the dialog.

"That their daughter is flying to a different country and spending some time with a man that she's not yet married to. Not to mention that they are visiting this man's brother?"

"This man's brother is me. And no they don't mind." Daniel stopped to look at her. "I don't get it. Sunil told me the Bollywood movies you all watch nowadays are quite progressive. I'm surprised this is actually an issue."

"It is not an issue. And yes they show it in the movies, but I have never known anyone who participates in this, um, type of activity."

Daniel's face registered an odd expression. One that Aahna couldn't quite read. She was worried for a moment that the innocence he once found charming was turning more into ignorance.

"Listen I am sorry. I should not have said anything. Tell me about your brother and his future wife. What are your plans with them?"

Daniel hesitated for a moment, but then continued walking. Aahna kept her pace next to him.

"I was thinking of taking them to the same places where you had initially brought me. And I spoke with Sunil about taking a few days off and touring around with them. Maybe going back up to the North again, visit Rajasthan, Agra. It'll be nice for all of us to see it together."

"That does sound like fun. And you will like those places."

Daniel paused. "I was also hoping that one night, you would join us for dinner."

This time Aahna stopped in her tracks. "You want me to meet your brother?"

"Sure, why not? We're pretty similar. I think you'd really like him."

"Isn't that a big step? I mean, in your world?"

"We live in the same world Aahna. You, me, Sunil, my brother, his fiancée."

"You know what I mean."

"It's not that big a deal. If you don't want to meet him, that's fine."

"I just mean, you and I haven't really gotten to spend much time together. Don't you think it's too soon to meet your family?"

"This is only because he's coming here soon. I can't stop that." Daniel shifted his laptop bag from one shoulder to the next. "As for you and me spending time together; let's try and fix that before he gets here." He smiled.

The now familiar flutter arose in Aahna's stomach. This was actually happening.

They reached the bus stop and stood a few feet behind the other waiting passengers.

"I should tell you that I don't know how to do this. You and I..." Aahna had trouble getting the words out. "I only know what I've seen in the movies." She didn't know why she was telling him this. Part of her wanted to set expectations, but the other part wanted to see his reaction. Would he would cut and run knowing the truth? To her surprise, Daniel smiled at her.

"You've already told me a bit about your life. I don't expect you to have the same level of experience that I would expect of a girl back home. I hope I don't offend you by saying that."

Aahna shook her head. "This doesn't make you want to rethink anything?"

"I told you already. You intrigue me. We'll figure everything else out. Together."

The bus pulled up and the awaiting passengers clambered onto the front, the side, the top, wherever they could find seats, or at least, a sufficient amount of space for their body.

Daniel nodded at Aahna as she made her way onto the bus. She pushed herself to the center, and tried and to peer out the windows as the bus pulled away. Daniel stood there, looking like a lighthouse in a torrential sea, amidst heavy clouds that would soon be approaching. She wondered how long the beam would remain, un-faltered and luminous; casting a light on an unpredictable wave she could never have known existed.

Chapter Six

The passengers streamed out of the main gates as flight after flight landed at Kolkata Airport. Outstretched hands waved furiously as family and friends recognized each other. The front doors to the airport were wide open just behind the main arrival gate, and the cool breeze wafted in providing relief to Daniel, who was trapped between an elderly gentleman who was too short to see anything, and a middle-aged, mustached man who continuously mistook every outgoing passenger for his long-lost relative, jumping up and down every five seconds. Everyone that came out of baggage claim looked the same to Daniel so he wasn't surprised at the gentleman's confusion. At least his two guests would be easily recognizable in this crowd.

Daniel checked his watch. Paul and Megan's flight had landed nearly forty-five minutes ago at one-thirty in the morning. He hoped they would come out soon, his excitement in seeing them trumping his creeping tiredness. He kept himself occupied by letting his eyes wander around the airport. The lights were incredibly bright, even for this time of night. Metal chairs lined the edges of the open area in front of him, where departing passengers checked their flights and hugged their relatives goodbye. Stores were all but closed for the most part, except for a small tea shop in the corner that still had a line-up. An older woman in a plain sari was bent over at one side, sweeping the day's debris into one pile. Daniel immediately thought of Aahna.

They had seen each other properly three times in the last week and a half and each time was even more stimulating than the last. The first time they had found an area in a nearby park where they sat sipping tea and chatting on an old wooden bench. Their conversations were quiet in tone, but the exchange was continuous. When one person finished a story, the other person followed up with a similar situation or an interesting question. Their chatter was seamless, and Daniel felt like he had known Aahna for more than the three months it had been since first laying eyes on her.

Daniel talked about his career aspirations, and openly discussed his father's never-ending need to judge and disapprove of everything the Harp boys did. He spoke highly of his mother and her unconditional, unwavering love. With his brother, he referred to their steadfast friendship, but also of the unspoken competition between them that challenged Daniel daily.

Aahna opened up about how her father's death affected her, especially when her mother and brother were so alike in their thinking. She explained how and when she was required to be married, and how she felt so alone when challenging them against the societal norms. Aahna mentioned Raina as well, and Daniel cringed at the thought that Aahna's life could turn out similarly.

The second night, Daniel suggested watching his first Bollywood movie. They snuck into the theater at the last minute so as not to attract attention, and chose a movie that had been out for a long time to avoid any significant crowds. The movie was a sub-titled comedy and Daniel laughed all the way through it. His exposure to musicals (which almost all Bollywood movies were) was slim, so he had to stop himself from making a face every time a song started and the location changed from a college in India to a mountain in Switzerland.

Daniel and Aahna shared popcorn, and their fingers brushed against each other every so often. The spark was magnetic, even in such a small touch, and Daniel felt like he was thirteen again, on a first date with a cute girl. Everything was simple and every glance represented a dozen different highs. He purposefully pretended to not understand a couple of plotlines and leaned over to Aahna to ask unnecessary questions. Her scent was intoxicating but not overpowering, like a mix of a rose garden and baby powder, although Daniel hadn't been exposed to either in a long time. When she leaned back over to explain something, her hand grazed his arm and for a moment she let it linger there. Ten minutes later, Daniel made up another question at the exact same time Aahna started to say something. They leaned into each other and their misstep caused them to be face to face. He was only inches away from her now, and there were no witnesses behind them. Any other date with this much electricity and a kiss would have been inevitable. But another song blared out of the speakers causing the tender moment to pass just as quickly as the location change on the screen.

Prior to the third meeting, Daniel's excitement at seeing Aahna was reaching new heights. It was as if the restrained demeanor of their relationship was increasing the intensity in his feelings. The plan was for Daniel to bring Aahna to a café frequented by tourists, so as not to attract attention from any locals. The café was far enough from Aahna's neighborhood, allowing both of them to not worry about anyone recognizing her and spreading the news-worthy gossip back to her village. The other restaurant patrons ignored the couple, most of them on laptops planning their next excursions or chatting happily and loudly in English. Daniel recognized German, Spanish and British accents predominantly, with a few American and Canadian tourists thrown in.

He had met a few of them on his previous visits to the café and they were a friendly bunch, as most travelers were.

Daniel and Aahna shared a slice of chocolate cake and each had a small espresso, Aahna's first, he learned. She asked him about the upcoming arrival of Paul and Megan, and the story of how they had met and fallen in love. Daniel explained the relatively mediocre and unromantic story - Paul had picked up Megan after a corporate soccer game - but Aahna was on the edge of her seat.

"Was it love at first sight?" she had asked.

"I don't think so. Megan thought Paul was too shallow and she turned him down twice before agreeing to go out with him," Daniel replied matter-of-factly.

The news hadn't appeared to faze Aahna in the least; in fact she wanted to hear about how all of Daniel's friends had met their significant others, so Daniel tried to recall all of the scenarios as best he could. But his gender's stereotypical need for succinctness got the best of him, resulting in glib recitations - he met her at a club; she used to date his friend; they hooked up at work - and Aahna herself started to look bored and saddened that people who were allowed to have such romantic lives could end up with a spouse they had met after getting drunk one night.

"How do your parents feel about all of these girls?" Aahna asked, almost shyly.

Daniel paused, feeling the need to tread carefully.

"They don't meet all of the girls of course," he started. "But they've been welcoming to anyone I have brought home." Daniel thought about his father in that moment. What exactly would Richard say if he met Aahna? The fear his father had about Daniel acclimating was now warranted. An uneducated cleaning lady from a third world country would hardly be a cause of celebration in the Harp household.

And Daniel knew even Sophia would be hard-pressed to find the positive light. He pushed the thoughts away, and turned his attention back across the table.

Daniel was still hopeful at the end of the date, when he proposed an evening walk around a deserted area near the café. Aahna appeared nervous at this suggestion, as if she finally realized Daniel was going to make a move. Truth be told, she was right. Daniel was trying to find a right time and place to kiss her, at the very least. It had been on his mind for days, and at a point in the relationship where he would normally be crawling out of a girl's bed looking for his clothes, he found himself hesitant to take even the smallest step. He didn't want to scare her, but he also didn't want her to think that friendship was his only interest. If he could whisk her off to a waterfall in Africa where they could be joined by a hundred backup dancers, but alas, it was just the two of them, standing around the corner from the café with only the streetlamp and a half-sleepy dog as their witnesses.

"Did you decide if you want to meet Paul?" Daniel had asked.

"Yes, I have heard so much about him that I am actually looking forward to meeting him," Aahna had replied.

"Excellent. He arrives in a couple of days so let's try and have dinner before we leave for the trip." The thought of leaving Aahna for ten days saddened Daniel and he could tell from her expression that she wasn't keen on the idea either.

"Okay, I will see what excuse I can come up with for that evening."

"So I guess no walk then?"

"I should head home. It is getting late."

"I'll put you in a taxi. My treat," Daniel had suggested.

Aahna smiled at him; that familiar, sweet smile that caused Daniel to reciprocate willingly each and every time.

They were silent. Even the dog had fallen asleep resulting in a quietness that Daniel rarely experienced in this boisterous city. This was the moment, he thought. No random rickshaw driver lurking around, no nosy store owners peering out their windows, no elderly couples going for walks.

He leaned in slightly and bent his head down. She didn't wear heels and was over half a foot shorter than he was. It was never more apparent than in this second. Aahna looked up at Daniel, with what he hoped was expectancy rather than fear. She closed her eyes and tilted her head up. He hesitated no longer and the kiss that had been lingering in the air for months was finally sealed. Her lips were soft, and he pulled her towards him. She was rigid for a moment, but then released the tension and drew her arms around his neck. They stayed in that position for several seconds, basking in the closeness. He felt her pull back and Daniel freed her from his grasp. Her arms fell to the side and she took a slight step back. What appeared to be calmness a moment ago suddenly turned into a shudder. Aahna glared at Daniel, as if seeing him for the first time. She put her hand to her mouth and for a second Daniel feared she would run off.

"Aahna," he said quietly.

She kept staring at him and Daniel had no idea how to gage her reaction. Finally, she put her hand down.

"*Thank you*," she practically whispered.

Daniel raised an eyebrow. That, he was not expecting. There was only one way to respond to that.

"No," he said. "Thank you." The lips that were just touching Aahna's turned into a smile.

Aahna grinned back, as if it finally dawned on her that she was the heroine in this romantic story.

"Daniel!" a female voice yelled loudly. The sound brought Daniel back to the present, with the noise of people around him, the bright lights, and the understanding that he was still standing in the middle of the airport. He looked up to pinpoint the familiar voice.

Sure enough, a petite, red-haired girl lugging a large worn out suitcase and a backpack appeared from around the corner, with a taller, blond haired, blue-eyed man directly behind her. Daniel's identical blue eyes rested on his brother and suddenly he too became like every other waiting family member. His arm shot out and he waved it aggressively to overpower the people around him and attract Paul and Megan's attention. They waved back as Daniel pushed his way through the crowd and to the front of the barricade, ecstatic to see a familiar face.

The two brothers exchanged hearty hugs and slaps on the back, while Megan reached up and gave Daniel a quick peck on the cheek. The rest of the crowd seemed fascinated by the trio and stopped waving and searching for their family members.

"You'll have to go around but I'll meet you out in front," Daniel said as he gestured towards the parking lot.

They nodded and turned away from him, walking around the crowd to the main doors.

Daniel took a deep breath as he headed outside, trying to get Aahna out of his mind and instead focus on the long awaited arrival of his brother.

He thought back to the moment when she had taken a step back from their kiss, as if realizing in a split second how such a small gesture could change her entire life. In fact, it had changed his.

***

The taxi chugged along the main road with its three passengers. The streets were deserted at this time of night. All of the millions of people Daniel encountered daily appeared to have vanished.

Where, he could not say. Only a few dogs fighting in the middle of the street could be seen and heard, along with a handful of homeless men that were sleeping under newspapers and torn, dirty blankets on the sides of the streets. The normally occupied sidewalks of fresh fruits and vegetable stands were all packed up and Daniel noticed the concrete pavements for the first time.

"It's so quiet," Paul mused from the backseat.

"I know, I've never even seen it like this," Daniel responded.

"You're not out every night clubbing?" Megan teased.

"Hardly. I'm always so drained from work I can't even imagine partying."

"It's a good thing we came along when we did then," Paul leaned forward in his seat. "Although I have to say, it feels a little weird to not be wearing a seatbelt."

"I know!" Megan exclaimed. "What's up with that?"

"It's mostly the older taxis. All the new cars have them," Daniel explained. "Whether or not they're used is a different story."

The light from the streetlamps gave the city a sepia colored tone. Almost everything was blanketed in this dim light and Daniel barely recognized the city he had been living in for the last three months.

"Did Dad give you a hard time about coming here?" he asked, looking back at his brother.

"Of course. But in all honesty, there were a lot of vaccinations we had to take. My arm was sore for 2 days."

"Stop being such a baby," Megan said, playfully hitting her fiancé in the arm. "It's a small price to pay for being here! Paul, we're in India!"

Daniel smiled at Megan's enthusiasm. He had always been fond of his soon-to-be sister-in-law. He remembered the numerous times the three of them had stayed up late, just chatting about anything. Megan hadn't judged Daniel after his break-up with Kelly, even though the two girls had become friends. She had also opted to stay mute on any milestones in Kelly's life since then, and he was grateful for that. Daniel wanted Kelly to be happy; he just didn't want to hear about it.

"What's the plan once we get to the hotel?" Paul asked.

"Sleep of course. It's almost the middle of the night," Daniel responded.

"Not for us, it's only mid-afternoon."

"I don't care. I'm going to sleep and you guys can entertain yourselves for the next few hours." Daniel turned back to face the front and rested his head against the leather seat, staring out the window as the small buildings whizzed by him.

***

The next morning, Daniel knocked on Paul and Megan's hotel room door. His plan was to take them out for breakfast and then show them his office. But first he wanted to tell them about Aahna, figuring the privacy of the hotel room was the best place to do this.

Megan opened the door. Her hair was wrapped up in a towel and she was sporting the terrycloth bathrobe provided by the hotel. "I'll be ready in ten minutes," Megan assured Daniel.

"Yeah, I've never heard that before," Daniel said, walking into the hotel room. The bed was unmade and two large suitcases were opened on the floor with clothes spilling out. The light was on in the bathroom and he could hear the sound of the electric razor.

"Make yourself at home," Paul yelled from the bathroom. "Sorry we're running late. We fell asleep like two hours ago so we're a bit out of it."

"Don't worry about it," Daniel said, as he pulled out the desk chair and sat down. "There's something I wanted to talk to you guys about before we headed out."

Paul came out of the bathroom as Megan removed the towel from her head and shook out her wet hair.

"Is it a cultural crash course?" Paul asked as he sat on the edge of the bed. Megan joined him.

"Not quite," Daniel answered. He took a deep breath, having no idea how his brother and Megan would take the news.

"I've been seeing someone," he started slowly. He looked at both Paul and Megan to gage their reaction.

"That's great," Megan said smiling. "Why do you look so freaked out?"

"She's not like other girls," Daniel answered.

Paul raised an eyebrow. "What do you mean by that?"

"She's the office, um, maid," Daniel managed to get out.

For a moment Paul and Megan didn't say anything. Daniel looked at them back and forth, hoping for a response soon.

"When you say maid...," Paul's voice trailed off.

"I mean, she cleans houses during the day and our office during the evening. That's how we met."

"Okaaaay," Megan said quietly. "Is it serious?"

"Yeah. Yeah. Yes," Daniel repeated.

Paul remained quiet.

"How long?" Megan asked.

"Not that long actually, but it's different with her," Daniel explained. "I mean we've only had a few dates, but we have this intense connection."

Megan looked at Paul, who still sat quietly.

"Well I'm happy for you," she said, turning back to face Daniel. "You've been so down and unsure lately that I'm glad there's someone out there that is making you happy."

Daniel smiled at Megan, knowing he could always count on her for support. But there was an ache in his stomach as he realized Paul had still not said anything. He looked at his brother, trying to read any signs, but the face that looked back was blank.

Megan put her hand on Paul's knee. "We're happy for him, right Paul?" Her voice was forceful as she tried to get Paul out of his trance.

Paul blinked, as if realizing where he was all of a sudden. He moved Megan's hand and got up from the bed. He headed to the bathroom and then turned around looking at his older brother. He looked like he was about to say something, then stopped and turned around back towards the bathroom again. He walked in and slammed the door behind him.

"Christ, what's his problem?" Daniel said, getting up from the chair.

Megan too, appeared perturbed. "I have no idea."

The bathroom door swung open and Paul stepped out. "What are you thinking?" he finally said. "Of all the things you could do here, you fall for a maid? Is this how you're planning on getting over Kelly? By breaking another girl's heart?"

Daniel was taken aback. He had expected some hesitation from his younger brother, but not this level of antagonism. He was about to speak but Paul hadn't finished yet.

"You want to have some fun here. I get it. But this has no future and I have a feeling that if this maid's family found out, you'd be in some serious trouble. I don't think they take lightly to their daughters hooking up with foreigners who are just going to leave them."

"What makes you think I'm going to leave her?"

"Well you're certainly not going to move here are you?" Paul looked his brother squarely in the eyes.

"She could come back with me."

At this announcement, even Megan looked surprised. "Come back with you? How would that even work?"

"I haven't thought everything through yet. But I didn't think I needed to run down all of my plans with you guys. I just wanted to tell you what's been going on here."

"Daniel you can't do this. A maid? Seriously?" Paul exclaimed again.

"Aahna," Daniel said quietly. "Her name is Aahna."

"What difference does it make what her name is?"

"Paul, stop it,"   Megan said. "This isn't your decision or even your problem."

"It's not a problem!" Daniel said, trying to keep his tone down. "I'm telling you as a courtesy. I'm not asking either of you for your permission. And could you sound anymore like Dad right now?"

Paul shook his head. "Don't even get me started on what Dad will say! I'm trying to prevent this from ever reaching his ears! If you want to have some fun here, date someone else. There are plenty of girls in this city who aren't maids. You could bring any of those girls back to Canada if things got serious. But why her? Why a maid?"

"I didn't pick her from a lineup!" Daniel said, his voice rising again.

"Don't give me that. You know very well you did. I highly doubt she decided to pursue you. You went after her and now you're stuck."

"I'm not stuck. True, I haven't worked everything out yet. But I'm happy. Happier than I've been in a long time. And it's because of Aahna."

For a moment there was silence. The three stood in a triangle, all with different stances. It reminded Daniel of the time he had told the two of them about the break-up with Kelly. Megan had been somewhat sympathetic, but Paul had yelled at him for a long time.

It was Megan who had been the voice of reason back then, and it was she who spoke first to break the silence now. "What if she doesn't want to come back with you?" she asked quietly.

Daniel looked at her. He hadn't even contemplated that angle. Was that even a possibility, he thought, quickly noticing the arrogance of his ways.

"She would have to give up everything wouldn't she?" Megan continued. "I would imagine her family wouldn't approve. And her life, well her life would be so hard in Canada. I'm thinking she's not educated, so it would be hard for her to get a job. I don't know how well she speaks the language, but I guess she could learn that. And your parents? What would your parents say?"

Daniel remained silent, glaring at Megan. He didn't want to hear any of this, even if it was all relatively accurate. Truth be told, he hadn't wanted to think of anything realistic. He was finally getting to enjoy the fun part of being in a relationship, and Daniel was hesitant to think ahead even two days, let alone two months, when it would be almost time for him to go home.

"Have whatever fun you want to have here," Paul said. "But leave it behind here. And don't get this poor girl's hopes up that you're going to whisk her off and provide her with some fairytale life in Canada. It's not going to happen."

Daniel was done talking about this. His brain was spinning with everything Paul and Megan had thrown at him. He sat back down on the chair, almost exhausted from the fight.

Megan came over to him and placed her hand on his shoulder. "You said yourself that you've only had a few dates with Aahna. Maybe just end it now then, before anyone gets hurt."

Daniel looked up at Megan. That thought hadn't even crossed his mind.

"I'd like to believe I'm a pragmatic romantic," Megan continued.

"How?" Daniel asked.

"You can't control who you fall in love with. But you can control who you spend the rest of your life with."

The words hit Daniel hard. He focused his eyes on a stain in the carpet in front of him. His hands were beginning to feel clammy, as if he was getting sick. Marriage? Is that what Aahna expected? Did all girls just think about marriage as soon as they met a guy? He gulped.

Daniel knew he had serious feelings about Aahna, but he hadn't yet attached those feelings to anything tangible. Jesus, what was he doing? Was he really going to be responsible for another broken heart?

"I wanted you to meet her," Daniel said, when he was finally able to find his voice.

Paul sighed. "We can meet her, if it'll make you happy. But I'm not on board with any of this. And frankly I think you're just leading her on."

Daniel continued to stare at the stain, not even realizing what words were coming out of his mouth. He was tired and wanted to go back to his room to lie down. He had been on such a high with Aahna for the last few days and now all of it was tumbling down with the arrival of his brother, the realist apparently. He rubbed his forehead. Was he just leading Aahna on? Was she expecting a long term plan that Daniel hadn't even contemplated yet? His shoulders felt heavy under the weight of Megan's compassionate hand. He wanted them both to leave. To go back to Canada, and leave him here, naïve but happy.

Daniel finally got up from the chair. "Let's figure this out later," he said. "You're on vacation, let's go get some food."

***

The air was humid as the trio made their way out of the Planetarium, their final stop for the day out in Kolkata. The fight from earlier was still in the air but Paul had been nothing but kind and warm to all of Daniel's co-workers when they had stopped by to visit TargetLife after breakfast. The plan for the day had been for Daniel to take his guests on a similar tour as Aahna had taken him. He sincerely hoped that a day out with the city's inhabitants would make Paul and Megan more receptive to their planned dinner with the now controversial Aahna.

It was almost seven in the evening and Daniel and his guests were scheduled to meet Aahna once again at **Bar-B-Q Land**. He was secretly hoping that the sheer amount of food would distract Paul from engaging in too much conversation with her. He wanted them to get along, that was a given. But after the reaction this morning, Daniel wasn't sure if any of this was a good idea. It was too late to back out, and he could imagine what Aahna would think if he did, so he had no other choice but to take a deep breath, and lead Paul and Megan into the restaurant.

The lights were just as bright as the first time, but there were more people in the restaurant now as it was a weeknght. Young employees from the nearby buildings were joking around and chatting loudly. Groups of guys and girls swarmed the buffet and continuously went outside for a quick smoke. Amidst all of the commotion, Daniel looked towards the back of the restaurant and his eyes locked on Aahna. The anxiousness on her face was apparent from where Daniel was standing. She had dressed up for the occasion, and looked no different than the dozen or so corporate girls that were milling around the restaurant. A waiter was approaching her with a jug of water, and she fended him off, her eyes now locked on Daniel. He nodded at her, and then began to lead his group towards the back.

For Daniel, the journey to the back of the restaurant seemed never ending. His knees had suddenly taken on a feeble approach to walking and the pit of his stomach was acting in a way he had never experienced before. He knew that Paul's opinion wasn't entirely prevalent at the end of the day, but he also knew how fragile Aahna was in their relationship. Any initial contention and he was worried she would bolt for the door. These thoughts raced through his head as the group finally made their way to Aahna's table.

"Hey…," Daniel said awkwardly and slowly as Aahna stood up. She smiled at him but made no additional motion to embrace or kiss him. Daniel had other thoughts. He squeezed her left hand and then turned to face his judging panel.

"Paul, Megan, this is Aahna."

A series of handshakes followed alongside uncomfortable looking smiles as the two couples sat down at the table. Paul immediately flagged down a waiter and ordered a single malt scotch. After it arrived, he threw it back, ordered another one, and placed his arm around his fiancée's chair.

"Do you come here often?" Megan asked to start the conversation. She spoke slowly and enunciated her words to a peculiar level.

Daniel rolled his eyes at her ignorance, but Megan continued to look across the table.

"I have come here a few times before, once with Daniel. The food is delicious," Aahna responded. No one seemed to be able to follow up with any further small talk so the foursome picked up their menus and began scanning the options.

The silence in the air was palpable. A waiter came by to fill up the water and Daniel felt that even that process seemed to take minutes, when only seconds had passed. Paul, meanwhile, ordered his third drink.

"So how did you spend your day?" Aahna finally asked.

Daniel breathed a sigh of relief. A safe topic.

Paul looked up from his menu, as if noticing her for the first time. Megan, who had been taught at a young age to always be polite to everyone, jumped in.

"Our day was fantastic!" Megan enthused. "We actually ended up going around to a lot of the places you showed Daniel earlier. I think I just enjoyed walking around though, if only because that's how you can truly soak everything in."

"Remember that security guard at Victoria Memorial? The one that was checking everyone's bags and acting like none of us knew how to use zippers?" Daniel said, turning to Aahna. "He was there again, and this time I realized he reminded me exactly of my dad!"

"You're totally right!" Megan piped in. "I didn't even think of that, but he does look just like Richard!"

Everyone but Paul laughed. He had already pounded back his drink and was looking around for the waiter again.

"Daniel has told me a lot about your father. He sounds like quite the strict man," Aahna said.

"Oh you have no idea!" Megan said. "I thought I had made a complete fool of myself the first time I met him. I'm surprised he let Paul and I continue dating."

"My father likes you Megan," Paul finally spoke up. "And he doesn't decide who I date."

"I didn't mean it like that...," Megan's voice trailed off.

At a nearby table, laughter ensued loudly creating a sharp juxtaposition to the bitter silence at table three. Daniel wondered if others in the restaurant could sense the mounting tension. He was beginning to feel irked by Paul's attitude and was realizing that perhaps the dinner was a bad idea. On top of that, the waiters were taking their sweet time bringing over any food for the foursome to distract themselves. It was as if they had figured out the dynamics of the table at the back of the restaurant and were avoiding it at all costs.

Paul took a sip of water and then folded his hands on the table. He looked directly at Aahna. "Speaking of family, do your parents know about my brother?"

"Paul," Daniel warned.

"What? I think it's a fair question."

Daniel glanced over at Aahna. "You don't have to answer that."

"It is okay. Your brother is right, it is a fair question." Aahna looked over at Paul. "My father passed away many years ago. It is just my mother, brother and I. And no, they are not aware of Daniel."

Paul looked down at his hands. "I'm sorry about your father. I didn't know." This time Megan glared at Paul. "Now, don't take this the wrong way, but what exactly is the end game here?" Paul continued.

"Christ," Megan mumbled under her breath.

"That's enough," Daniel said.

"I'm serious," Paul said. "I'd like to know what the plan is here for you two. Is this just for fun? Or do I need to start shopping for best man attire?"

"You're drunk," Megan hissed. "Just stop it."

"Don't be ridiculous. I'm just stating things as I see them. My older brother has finally found himself in this glorious country." Paul locked his hands behind his head. He smiled wryly across the table.

Daniel fumed from across the table. For a moment he felt that he was sitting across from his father, and no longer the younger brother that he had been so proud of. He would never have imagined such an adverse reaction to Aahna. Not from someone who had been as open-minded as him, and not from someone who should have just been content to see his brother happy. He was certain the alcohol wasn't helping either.

The four of them sat in tense silence for over a minute. Finally Aahna stood up from the table and excused herself to the ladies room. When she was out of earshot, Daniel threw his menu down on the table.

"What has gotten into you?" he proclaimed at his younger brother. "Why are you treating her this way? She has done nothing wrong."

"Maybe she hasn't, but you certainly have," Paul responded.

"Why are you so against this?"

"Because I don't understand the point of it!" Paul hissed. "Neither of you are saying this is just for fun. If you were, I wouldn't bat an eye. But instead, you're both sitting here like you've found your long lost soul mate. You're one of the most pragmatic people I know yet you're acting like this is completely normal."

"Why can't it be?" Daniel asked while trying to control the waver in his voice.

"It just isn't!"

"Guys," Megan interjected. "We should talk about this elsewhere."

"No, Megan," Daniel said. "I really want to know what has your fiancé so hot and bothered." He looked Paul square in the eye, the shape, size and color of which mimicked his own.

Paul didn't say anything for a moment. He rubbed his hand against his chin, as if formulating his thoughts. His jaw unclenched slowly and the alcohol-induced redness in his cheeks gave him a more childish expression, like a young boy who had just come inside after playing in the snow.

"You've had a hard last few years," he started calmly. "You need to find someone that you can spend your life with. And being with Aahna, while exhilarating and exotic and fascinating now, is only going to make the rest of your life harder. There is no positive outcome to this situation. Not for her and her family, and certainly not for you. I just…," his voice trailed. "I just don't want to see you broken again."

Daniel focused on the placemat in front of him. The corners of the bamboo woven table setting were beginning to fray. He picked at it with his fingers, not knowing how to respond. Aahna still hadn't returned to the table and Daniel was worried that she was somewhere crying.

"Can you go check on her please?" he asked Megan.

She nodded and got up quickly from the table, glancing back at Paul.

Daniel leaned forward on the table and clasped his hands. "To be honest, I don't actually know what I'm doing. I can only go by what I feel. And this feeling is different than anything that has come before it."

"Being in a different country can do that," Paul said, only half-jokingly.

"I need to see this out, whatever that means. I need it to run its course." Daniel leaned back in his chair. "And most importantly, I need my brother to be happy for me."

Paul sipped his water. After a long pause, he finally nodded. "Yeah, okay. I can try."

"That's all I ask."

"For what it's worth, she seems to really like you."

Daniel leaned forward. "Paul, I think I might..."

"Chicken, sir?" A loud voice burst through as suddenly three wait staff appeared with steaming hot dishes.

Daniel, caught off guard, could only nod as the waiters put the dishes down in front of the brothers. The aroma was mesmerizing from the chicken, goat and lamb dishes, their spices blending together in perfect harmony.

At the same time, Aahna and Megan arrived back from the ladies room, and for a mere moment there was a sense of normalcy at table three. It seemed like two girls had just finished re-applying their makeup and were headed back to their awaiting partners.

Paul nodded at Megan as she sat back down, as if to say that the issues were resolved, at least for the short term.

Aahna slid into the seat next to Daniel and smiled at him, the same smile that made all of the drama worth it to him. "It looks like I came at the right time," she said, glancing at the food.

Daniel watched as she tucked a piece of hair behind her ear. "Yes, yes you did," Daniel replied.

***

The TargetLife office was in full swing when Daniel arrived at work the next morning. He arrived later than normal due to his restless sleep from the night before. Although he and Paul had resolved their issues somewhat, Daniel was having a hard time forgetting about the confrontation. He couldn't help but wonder if Paul was right. What was the end game in all of this? Both he and Aahna hesitated in speaking about any future plans, mostly because they didn't have any, and saying this fact aloud would only make the current situation unbearable.

Daniel was content in the fact that any major decisions regarding the future wouldn't have to be made for at least another two months. In the meantime, he vowed to just enjoy himself in this newfound relationship. Daniel began to feel better about his situation as he headed to his desk and took out his laptop. He leaned back in his chair and stared out the window. Outside, the main open area between the office buildings was relatively deserted, as most employees had already begun their day. A slight breeze lifted a plastic bag from the ground and spun it around. Daniel looked on as the bag gently flew up and down until finally landing a few feet away. He almost closed his eyes for a moment when he felt a presence next to him.

"Long night?" Sunil asked. His tone sounded friendly as he looked down at his colleague.

"You could say that," Daniel replied. "How are you?"

"I'm fine. We're going to need to chat this morning. Do you have some time now?"

Daniel nodded and got up from his dream-like state to follow Sunil into the corner office.

Sunil's desk was filled with piles of paper and supplies that were haphazardly thrown about. It was surprising for someone who completed ninety percent of his work on a computer, Daniel thought to himself.

"First of all, I wanted to say how grateful we are for all the work that you've accomplished since your arrival," Sunil started.

Daniel paused in front of the chair he was just about to sit on; realizing quickly that this conversation wasn't going to be as trivial as the rest of their meetings.

"We're doing so well in fact, that your boss has agreed to let you go back to Canada early!" Sunil smiled widely at Daniel. "We're going to be sorry to see you go, but I imagine you're ecstatic to be headed home."

Daniel stared through Sunil, suddenly feeling like the plastic bag that was swept away uncontrollably just moments earlier. His throat felt dry and his hands clammy. He looked over at the desk, and then down at his hands, and then back up again. The words Sunil had said were heard, but not fully processed. Could this be happening? Daniel realized quickly that Sunil was expecting a response. "I had no idea that was even an option," he managed to sputter out.

"Neither did I. But you can imagine that keeping you here unnecessarily is costly so if the work is no longer required, it would make sense to send you back." Sunil leaned forward. "I'm a little confused why you don't look overly happy about this."

Daniel managed to force a smile. "I am happy, really. Just caught off guard I suppose."   "Understandable. I know you have a trip planned with your brother. I want you to go on that and then stay on a couple of more days here to wrap everything up. After that, it's home sweet home for you." Sunil leaned back and grinned.

Daniel sat still. The words were jumbling around in front of his face and even though Sunil had finished talking, his voice was still resonating in the office. He thought back to ten minutes ago, when he had made peace with prolonging any serious decision making. Sometimes the hardest decisions are the ones that are made for you, he thought. For now though he had to leave professionally, lest Sunil delve deeper into Daniel's hesitation. He got up slowly. "It's going to be

odd to not come here every day," he managed to get out. "I'm so used
to everything now."

Sunil nodded. "We will miss having you around. But no matter!
You are still here for a little while longer so we will have a proper
goodbye then."

Daniel nodded back and headed out the office door, his mind
still reeling. Back at his desk, he could barely focus. His laptop was
lighting up with continuous emails but nothing registered in his head.
He looked out of the window again. The plastic bag was still there, now
caught between the rungs of a park bench. Daniel sighed and closed
the lid on his laptop. It was giving him a headache. He looked across
the office at all the staff going about their workday. His eyes landed on
a desk near the main entrance and he recalled the time he was working
late one day and a girl had been dusting the desk. Their eyes had met
briefly, but that was all that mattered. He was so entranced he had
followed her into the kitchen just to see her again. He knew now, like
he knew then, that he would have followed her anywhere. But that was
the heart speaking, and only the heart.

His practical mind remained ignorant of anything he was truly
feeling. On paper the next steps were clear. Say goodbye to Aahna,
and return to his life back in Canada. Years from now, he could tell his
grandchildren about the great love affair he encountered in an exotic
land, far, far away. Of course that was easier said than done. He wasn't
ready to give up on his relationship with Aahna, and he could only
imagine how devastated she would feel upon hearing the news.

He placed his head in his hands. Paul had been right. What in
the world had he been thinking? Daniel jumped out of his seat and
headed to the men's room. He threw cold water on his face and stared
at himself in the mirror. His eyes were swollen from the lack of sleep
and his hair was disheveled, a far cry from its usual style.

He just needed more time; that was all. To figure out a plan that would be favorable for everyone. Even as he thought about it, he realized the point was moot. Unless one of them drastically changed their lifestyle, there was no easy answer. And drastically changing your lifestyle for a person you had only known a few months went against everything he believed in. His life was planned, organized and rational. Those were the facts.

He looked at himself in the mirror again and shook his head. Daniel hadn't met Aahna's family yet but he could only imagine how they would react to any kind of news about him. The likely scenario was that irrespective of everything, he was headed back on a plane to Canada, and that too, alone. Attempting to discuss anything else with Aahna's family would only put her in harm's way and he couldn't leave her to deal with the consequences by herself.

There it was; he thought to himself. A decision made. Daniel took a deep breath and exhaled slowly. Now it was just a matter of telling her the same thing.

He turned away from the mirror and headed towards the door. As his hand reached the handle, a realization formed over him. A realization that had started to surface as soon as Sunil had made his announcement moments earlier. Daniel shook off the feeling. He knew deep down that he was doing the right thing. He also knew that there was no other solution. His home was thousands of miles away, and hers was here. But the truth still lay there, like the plastic bag that was waiting for another breeze to come and take it away. To pry it free from the cold iron bench. Something he knew now he could never admit to her.

I am in love with her, he finally said to himself. I know that to be true.

Chapter Seven

Aahna stepped off the bus as the warm breeze lifted her shawl slightly and made the loose hairs around her face flutter. She heaved her bag higher onto her shoulder and headed in the direction of her house. She hadn't spoken to Daniel today and it made her heart uneasy. His desk had been tidied and his lamp was off by the time she had arrived for work. He would be leaving for his trip with his brother in a couple of days and she wanted to make sure they were able to meet prior to that. Since the night before, when the four had gone for dinner, Aahna's mind and heart were racing. She knew her and Daniel's relationship was fragile at best, and the thought of his brother's incessant objections into his head worried her.

Aahna wasn't sure what to make of Paul. She had liked Megan, who had seemed far more down-to-earth and willing to accept Aahna as a possible friend. But Paul was different. In actuality, she had expected him to be very similar to Daniel, but was thrown off by his complete disregard of any potential future they may have.

The truth was that everything Paul had said was true. Whether or not Daniel wanted to admit it, the two of them had not once spoken about their future plans. He would be heading back to Canada soon enough, and no mention had been made of where that would leave her. She tried to think of their relationship as a short-term affair, one in which years from now she could look back at as a distant, happy memory. But any thought of a world where he didn't exist sparked a twinge inside of her she had never felt before. The idea of him had given her the audacity to lie to her family day in and day out. None of that was right, but the choice was not hers. She did not live in a world where the two parts could coincide, and until that day came, she was apt to enjoy them wholly, but separately.

Aahna had always wanted something more than the life she had been pre-destined to live. But now that the situation had presented itself, she was scared about the consequences. Was there no happy medium she could find? One where she was able to keep her family but still choose the person she wanted to spend the rest of her life with? She didn't even know if that person was Daniel. Aahna never really understood it when people said they could love someone until the day they die. How did they know that? All Aahna knew was that she couldn't imagine a day where she didn't love Daniel. Maybe that was the same thing, or maybe that was the more realistic way to look at things.

Aahna chuckled to herself as she walked by a furniture store and turned onto the alleyway that led to her house. There was nothing realistic about her current situation. If she was in a movie, either her or Daniel would blindly give up their entire lifestyles just to live with the other. But that situation was so extreme that neither person had brought it up as a possibility. Aahna pictured Daniel walking down the same alleyway and ducking his head into the doorway of her house. She pictured him sitting on the small cot next to her brother as they chatted about their day, while her mother continued to make dinner for everyone. Aahna shook her head at the ridiculousness of that scenario. She needed to accept the fact that Daniel was only meant to be here for a short term. And while she truly believed her destiny would provide her with greater things, she was beginning to realize that Daniel's purpose was to help her identify courage and move on. This thought caused the now repetitive pang in Aahna's stomach to re-appear.

Aahna's head began to hurt as the side effects of her emotional dilemma became stronger and stronger. She decided to push everything out of her mind for the rest of the evening as she neared her house. She would find Daniel tomorrow and confront him about their relationship. One way or the other, the two would have to come to a decision about their future, or lack thereof. Aahna felt slightly better at the thought of seeing Daniel the next day. She wondered when those feelings would start to subside; the addictive high when she saw him and the catastrophic low when she didn't. It was enough to make her lose her mind slowly, but apparently this feeling was one of the many definitions of love.

Aahna shifted her bag from one shoulder to the other as she turned onto the small street that led directly to her house. From afar, she could make out Raina sitting on her stoop, wringing her hands. Aahna's heart melted at the thought of her friend, and how she was probably sitting outside to allow her crazy husband to cool off. As she got closer, she saw the look of fright on Raina's face. It was more pronounced than normal, and Aahna suddenly got the sinking suspicion that this had nothing to do with Raina's husband.

Aahna slowed her walk at the same time that her friend jumped off the stoop and ran towards her.

"I had no choice!" Raina exclaimed as she grabbed both of Aahna's arms. It took Aahna only a few seconds to realize what Raina was talking about. She took a step back.

"What d-d-did you do?" Aahna managed to stutter.

Raina's face was flush. Her eyes were full of tears and a bruise was forming on her left cheek. "They were questioning me about where you were and I didn't know what else to say!"

"Who was questioning you?" Aahna demanded to know.

"Sourav. Your mother. You were not home again last evening and they suddenly decided to ask me about it today."

"I told them I went to the movies with Shibani," Aahna said. "Why would they ask you anything?"

"They didn't believe you," Raina replied. "They said you never used to go out this much and so they came to ask me if I knew anything."

"What did you say to them?" The heat was beginning to rise in Aahna's face. How much trouble was she in?

"At first, I told them that I didn't know anything. And that you had become really good friends with Shibani and she liked to go out a lot. They seemed to believe me, but..."

"But, what?"

"After your family left, Vikas started to beat me. He said that he didn't believe you were out with a friend. And then he said that if I knew anything about you I better say it now before the real truth came out." Raina's face crumpled. "Oh Aahna, I am so sorry. I just wanted the pain to stop. I had to tell Vikas everything, Aahna. And then he told your family."

Aahna stared at her friend's swollen face. Her surroundings began to move in slow motion. Raina's sobs sounded muffled. The bag that was on her shoulder dropped to her side. Her family knew the truth. And they had found out in the worst way possible. She had been careless, she knew that. But in every ounce of joy she was able to experience in the past few months, she had not expected this inevitability. She hadn't even mentally prepared herself for this moment. But here it was. Behind the closed doors of her small, comfortable house lay a mounting anger. She could almost sense the tension from the street where she stood numb.

Aahna's whole world was about to come crashing down, and she had no idea how her family, who had never had to experience this level of betrayal, was about to react.   She could vaguely hear someone calling her name. Aahna peeled her eyes away from the door to her friend who was still standing in front of her.

"You have to go inside," Raina said between sobs. "I think you have to just get this over with."

Aahna glared at Raina. She wanted to slap her across the face, to stop the sobs and tears that were streaming down. How dare she cry on her behalf? How dare she even try to explain herself? Raina had always been weaker than her, choosing to live with a man that abused her rather than run away and start a new life. Aahna had found that weakness endearing in a way. She wanted to be the older sister that could help guide Raina to a better life. But that trust was broken now. She could barely look at her. Aahna picked up the bag from the ground and made her way past Raina and to her house.   She paused at the doorway one more time. For a second she felt like bolting. Could she run away now to Daniel's hotel? To his arms? No, she thought to herself. That would make everything worse. She prided herself on being stronger than girls like Raina and now the situation where she had to prove it had presented itself. Aahna took a deep breath and pushed open the door to her house.

Inside it was silent. The stove was turned off, which was abnormal for this time of evening. A small kerosene lamp was flickering in the corner. The rest of the tiny house remained dark. It took a second for Aahna's eyes to adjust and realize that no one was actually sitting in the front room. She put her bag down, took off her shoes and headed towards the rear of the house, where three cots lay side by side. As she neared the back room, she could hear faint sobs. Aahna walked through the open doorway and finally came face to face with her family.

Aahna's mother was sitting on the cot farthest from the door, rocking herself back and forth. The sobs were hers. Sourav was sitting on the cot next to his mother, patting her on the back awkwardly and muttering to himself. Aahna stood in the doorway staring at the two of them. It was awful to watch her mother cry and know that she was the cause of it. Tears began to form slowly in Aahna's eyes as well. After a few seconds, Sourav looked up and finally noticed his sister standing there silently.

"Aahna," he said quietly. "What have you done?"

At the mention of Aahna's name, Ruma looked up at her daughter. There was a steady stream of tears, and her hands were trembling. Aahna could barely look her in the eye.

She hesitatingly stepped further into the room, not sure if she should sit or stand or run out the door and never look back.

"I can explain," she started.

"Is it true?" Sourav cut her off.

Aahna looked down at the ground. She jabbed the floor with her big toe as she tried to find the right words. Of course it was true. Aahna nodded, still unable to complete a thought in her head.

She heard her mother gasp and Aahna kept her head down in shame. She almost wished her family would start screaming at her. The quietness was unbearable.

"How could you let this happen?" Sourav continued. "Do you know how this makes you look?"

Aahna finally lifted her head. "Like I am willing to find my own path," she said defiantly.

"No, it makes you look like a whore," Sourav finished matter-of-factly.

It was Aahna's turn to gasp. The word hit her across the face, leaving a far more stinging effect than any slap could have. She closed her eyes, the tears now flowing freely.

"Do you know what people will say about us?" Ruma chimed in.

Aahna sat on the edge of a cot and put her head in her hands. Was that her mother's favorite argument about everything? Aahna brushed the tears from her face and wiped her hands on the sari, attempting to compose herself.

"With all due respect," Aahna said, "I do not want to start talking about what other people will think and say. To answer your question," she continued, looking directly at her brother. "I did not mean for this to happen nor did I plan it."

"You certainly didn't stop it did you?" Sourav retorted.

"Correct," Aahna responded.

Ruma continued sniffing in the corner. She used the corner of her sari to wipe her nose and kept rocking back and forth.

"Why are you so calm?" Sourav said, his voice rising. "Do you even understand what you have done?"

"I have not done anything," Aahna said, her voice matching Sourav's. "I have just befriended someone you don't approve of."

"Befriended??" her brother exclaimed. "Is that the word they are using nowadays?"

"I do not want to speak about the details of the relationship," Aahna replied calmly.

Suddenly Ruma leapt off the bed and was in front of her daughter in a second. The journey was so quick Aahna had no time to cower as Ruma's hand landed hard across Aahna's face.

"You do not want to speak of anything?" Ruma roared. "Not of this relationship, not of what other people will say. Tell me child, what do you want to speak about? How your father must be devastated from wherever he is? How you have shamed this family? How everyone in this neighborhood knows that you have been out and about with a foreign man. Who will marry you now Aahna? Who will want you?" Ruma's voice trembled. The tears were gone and all Aahna could see was pure rage in those eyes. The eyes that always seemed gentle and loving. The eyes that had looked at her with pride and happiness. All she saw now was a strange vacancy.

Aahna rubbed the part of her face where her mother's hand had just been.

"Is this man going to marry you?" Sourav asked. "Is he going to take you back to Canada and marry you? Or was he just having a little bit of fun while he was on vacation?"

Aahna cringed at how eerily similar her brother and Daniel's brother sounded in this moment. "I don't know if he will marry me. I don't know what our future is."

"How naïve can you be?" Ruma exclaimed. "I did not raise a daughter to believe in some fantasy love story. Why in the world would you think you can have any kind of future with this man?"

"Daniel," Aahna said quietly. "His name is Daniel."

The second slap hit her even harder than the first one. "Don't you dare say his name in my house," Ruma said. "I don't know what you have done with him, and I do not want to know. But you will quit that job immediately and stop seeing him."

"I can't do that Ma," Aahna said, her voice quivering. "Sunil got me that job and I have a responsibility to be there."

"Don't be ridiculous. When you explain to Sunil why you have to quit I am sure he will be more than happy to see you go."

"I won't tell him what happened."

"Tell him whatever you want but starting tomorrow Sourav will take you to all of your daytime jobs, and bring you right back home. You are not leaving this house unless one of us is with you at all times."

"For how long?" Aahna protested.

"Until your friend is gone."

Aahna looked back and forth between Sourav and her mother. They were both standing over her now and their faces were full of wrath. She had never seen them so enraged in all of her life. What did she expect though? That they would willingly open their arms to Daniel? That they would even listen to what she had to say?

"How do you know he will leave me?" Aahna asked bravely.

"Because men like him have no interest in girls like you," Sourav replied. "He can tell you whatever you want to hear right now, but make no mistake. As soon as he needs to, he will be on the first plane back to Canada with no thought of you."

"You don't know him," Aahna said. "He is different."

"Then who?" Sourav said. "Who are you comparing him to? What movie did you see this storyline in?"

Aahna put her head back in her hands, feeling hopeless. She wanted Daniel to appear out of nowhere and tell her everything would be okay. But she couldn't help listen to her family's words. How well did she really know Daniel? It had bothered her that they hadn't spoken about their future, but perhaps it was all intentional after all. Perhaps Daniel had no plans for the future with her, and this was just his way to enjoy some time in India. Her head began to hurt again, as it had before she headed home and ran into Raina.

"You are done with him, do you understand me?" Ruma said.

Aahna looked up at her mother. Whatever power she felt she had was being sucked away slowly. She was exhausted from all of the lying, and was almost relieved that her family knew the truth.

"Do you understand me?" Ruma asked again.

Aahna closed her eyes, pushing Daniel from her mind. She did the only thing that felt right in that moment. She nodded.

***

Aahna woke up the next morning feeling incredibly restless. She was unable to get any sleep, and her cheek still throbbed from her mother's double attack on her face. That pain was nothing however compared to the pain she felt in her heart. She was near grief-stricken over the prospect of losing Daniel and almost welcomed another slap in the face. Anything to distract her from a pain that couldn't be remedied. Rolling over to her side, Aahna stared at the concrete wall next to her. Tracing her finger over a mark in the wall, she moved from the smooth flawless surface to the indented nick. The nick, only a few inches in length gave way to the smooth portion of the wall. She felt that last night, her life had become that flawed part of the wall. If she held out long enough, the smooth surface that was once her previous life would surely appear again.

The door to the bedroom opened and Sourav poked his head inside. "Wake up. It's almost time for me to drop you off at Sunil's house." He shut the door again.

Aahna closed her eyes. Going to Sunil's would only remind her of the promise that she had made to her mother the previous night. She would need to come up with some excuse to Sunil about not being able to work in the office anymore, followed by an even more difficult conversation with Daniel. Aahna had no inkling what she would say to him, but she was tempted to hide from him and instead talk to him over the phone. Seeing him would no doubt make her lose her nerve and instead dive straight into his arms. Aahna got up slowly from the bed and hunted for her slippers. Wrapping her sheet around her body tighter, she headed into the front room. Her mother and Sourav were finishing their tea, neither of them talking. They glanced up when Aahna came in, but then simply went back to looking at their cups.

I did this, Aahna thought to herself. I caused this pain and tension. And for what? Because a good looking man looked at me twice? What would her father say? He wanted her to live out her dreams and go against the grain. But he would never have been all right with disrespecting the family like this. And that was what she had done. She deserved to be happy but could there have been a way to accomplish that without alienating her family? Maybe. Aahna had gotten swept up in a forbidden relationship without thinking through any consequences properly. And here she was face to face with her consequences, in the form of an angry young rickshaw driver, and a woman who had done nothing wrong except raise her children alone and want the best for them.

"I will tell Sunil today about the office job," Aahna informed her family. She looked down at her slippers, barely able to speak the next few words. "I am sorry, for all of this," she whispered.

"Just get ready. We are going to be late," Sourav said, rising from the floor. He brushed past his sister and headed into the bedroom without a second glance.

***

A short while later, Aahna and her brother found themselves in front of Sunil's apartment. She gazed up at the six story building and thought about how long she had been coming there to clean his apartment. Other than the time of her father's death, she hadn't missed any days, and usually looked forward to the morning banter with her old friend. But today was different. Today her heart ached more than it had in years, and all she wanted to do was go home and crawl into bed once again.

Reluctantly, she stepped out of the rickshaw, and without so much as a glance at her brother, she headed up the five flights of stairs to Sunil's apartment. As usual, Moumita was there to answer the door and bark out her instructions for the morning.

"When you're done with the shelves, all of the pantries need to be restocked and tidied up today," Moumita continued. She sauntered in front of Aahna while speaking and didn't appear to notice the melancholy look on her maid's face.

It took Aahna a few moments to realize that Sunil was nowhere to be found in the small apartment.

"Has Sir stepped out?" she asked casually.

Moumita turned around and looked at Aahna, as if surprised she hadn't already completed all of her tasks.

"He left for the office earlier than usual today," she said, taking a seat the kitchen table.

Aahna nodded and faced away from Moumita, keeping herself busy by dusting the front room's shelves. "He must be busy," she continued, hoping to sound nonchalant. In short, she was relieved. It meant not being able to tell Sunil yet that she would no longer work in the office. And if she wasn't able to tell him, it meant she would be required to show up to her office job later that day. Sure, Moumita could pass along the message to him, but Aahna conveniently ignored that possibility.

"He will be busy for the next few days," Moumita replied, sipping on her usual hot and spicy tea. "It would seem the Canadian is headed back to his homeland."

A truck suddenly slammed on its brakes on the street, screeching to a stop near the apartment and causing Moumita to look outside the window in fury.

In that exact moment, Aahna's duster collided with a small glass statue on the shelf, knocking it to its side. Aahna watched as the statue teetered on the edge, as if in slow motion, and then lost its balance, heading for the floor. She could make no move to reach for it. Her body had paralyzed. The glass statue made contact with the tiled floor and shattered instantly, dozens of its pieces flying everywhere.

Aahna dropped to the floor, barely even noticing the statue. Her hands rested against the cold tile and it was the second time in two days she felt the wind knock out of her. *It would seem the Canadian is headed back to his homeland.* The words repeated over and over in her head. How was this possible? He still had at least another month before making arrangements to head home. What had happened? She stared at the floor intensely, wanting it to answer all of her questions. A sharp pain started to surface on her right hand, causing Aahna to minimally disengage from the thoughts in her head and look down. She had landed directly on a piece of glass, and it was now protruding out of her skin with small droplets of blood beginning to spill.

"What happened?" Moumita exclaimed, appearing at her side. "You're bleeding!" Moumita ran into the bathroom and returned with a damp towel.

Aahna stayed perched on the floor, staring at her hand. She was for the most part, still in a daze as she watched the blood drip to the floor. Her brain was fixated on Moumita's revelation a few minutes ago, and it hadn't had time to register on the glass that had torn through her skin and made its way inside of her.

She allowed Moumita to pick her up gently off the floor and place her on a nearby chair. She looked away as Sunil's wife carefully removed the glass and began dabbing her hand with the towel to clean up the blood. Aahna peered at her as Moumita brought out two bandages and plastered them on to Aahna's hand. She had never liked

Moumita. But in this scenario of almost motherly tenderness, Aahna felt that for just a moment, she wasn't alone.

"Thank you," she whispered finally.

"Don't mention it," Moumita answered as she rocked back on her heels and got up to examine the glass on the floor. "I'll clean this up."

"No, please, it was my fault."

"You rest your hand. Anyone would have been startled by that truck outside," Moumita said, clearly not realizing that it was her own words that had caused the statue to break. She headed to her front closet and fished out the broom.

Aahna watched as Moumita brought the shards of glass together in one heap towards the center of the floor.

"You said that the Canadian was leaving. Do you know why?" Aahna asked. She felt brave all of a sudden. She needed to know the answers and for once she felt that Moumita might be sympathetic and actually speak to her properly.

"Sunil was vague about it. He just said all of the work and training was completed faster than they originally thought, and so he assumed Daniel would want to head back to Canada."

"Do you believe him?"

Moumita looked at Aahna in surprise. Then she laughed. "Of course I believe him. Why would he lie to me about this?"

Aahna looked down at her hand, realizing the truth. Sunil had found out somehow, she was sure of it. Either Daniel's driver had finally opened his mouth, or Daniel and Aahna had been spotted somewhere together outside of the office. It would be the only explanation for Daniel's sudden departure. She didn't buy the 'no more work' storyline. She couldn't explain why, but she felt that the truth was far more complicated. And she was certain that Sunil would never tell his wife of

Aahna's indiscretion. He was too attached to her family and would retain that loyalty.

"You can go home if you like," Moumita said, interrupting her thoughts. "You shouldn't really put any pressure on your hand so I'm all right with you leaving now."

Aahna barely let Moumita finish the last part of the sentence before grabbing her purse and running out the door. She had only one place she needed to go, especially if it was the last time she would go there.

***

"Mr. Harp," the voice appeared to be in the distance. Daniel was lost in thought once again, staring out his window and looking for another plastic bag to compare his life with.

"Sir?" the voice said again, this time sounding closer. Daniel looked up realizing that the voice was directed at him.

"Yes, sorry," he said.

"There is a young lady outside that claims she knows you." The gentleman who owned the voice looked slightly uncomfortable. "I think she works here, as one of the cleaning staff, but I must be mistaken. What could a maid want with you?"

Daniel, ignoring the man's last comment, jumped out of his chair and headed towards the elevator. It's not what she wants from me, he thought to himself. It's what I need from her. He pushed the elevator button several times in frustration, willing it to go down faster. He needed to see her right away, and that urgency overtook any thought of what he was actually going to say when he finally did.

The elevator lurched to a stop and Daniel hurried out the doors before they were even fully open. He jogged out of the lobby and into the hot air. It didn't take him long to spot her. She was sitting by herself on a bench in the far corner and he found himself quickening his pace. His breath was uneven at best, and the heat started to cause sweat beads on his face. He ignored all that and kept his eyes on the beautiful creature staring off into space. When he finally reached her, he stopped himself. His not knowing what to say finally caught up to him. Aahna got up slowly from the bench and turned to face him. Daniel's breathing began to steady itself and he opened his mouth to speak.

"You're leaving," she announced, before he could utter his first word. It was a statement. Not a question, barely an utterance. Just a fact.

Daniel looked at her in surprise. It had only been a day, how on earth could she have found out?

"Sunil's wife mentioned it to me," Aahna said, as if reading Daniel's thoughts.

"He's making me go," Daniel replied.

"He knows about us," Aahna said.

"I know."

Now it was Aahna's turn to look surprised.

"The work I was sent here to do isn't complete yet," Daniel continued. "I could tell as soon as he told me to leave that he had found out somehow."

"But this affects your job. He can't just send you back. You should talk to your boss."

"What's the point?" Daniel sighed, sitting on the bench. "He's a good man and he's only doing what he thinks is right. I've already caused enough problems here, I'm not about to get him into trouble."

Aahna sat down next to him.

"Besides, maybe we needed something like this to finally have the difficult conversation."

"I already had a difficult conversation last night," Aahna said, and she started to explain how her family had found out.

Daniel's eyes widened as she continued on with her story. Even though his own father was known to be strict, Daniel could never imagine this kind of reaction.

"Oh Aahna," he said, when she finished. "I feel awful that I wasn't there."

"You think that would have made it better?"

"No, but I should have been there. At least to defend you." Daniel stared at the tree in front of them, feeling too ashamed to look at Aahna. The full effect of everything she had sacrificed to be with him finally hit home. His family would be willing to overlook what they perceived to be a fling, but hers never would. In her family's mind, it had tarnished her completely. And there weren't enough words that Daniel could say to make it better.

"When are you leaving?" Aahna asked in a quiet voice.

"The secretary told me she was able to put me on Paul and Megan's flight. So basically the day after we get back from the tour." Daniel could feel Aahna's breath leave her body slowly.

"Aahna," he started, looking over at her finally. "I don't think you can come with me." Daniel's voice cracked.

Aahna looked at him, her eyes now glassy with the beginning formation of tears. "Oh Daniel," she said slowly. "I had no intention of leaving with you."

Daniel pretended to look relieved, but in actuality he was surprised. It wasn't arrogance that caused his surprise, but rather a genuine belief that Aahna felt as strongly about him as he did about her.

She must have realized by the look on his face that her words had come out harsher than expected. "I meant I can't leave my family.

I don't know anything about your country and I don't see how it could possibly work for us there. Do you?"

Daniel stayed quiet. He wanted for a moment to be completely honest with her. He ached to tell her that how he just wanted to run away some place together where they could both be equal partners and where no one would look at them differently. Where there was no disapproving families or nosy bosses. Where he could wake up each morning, look into the eyes of a great love, and start his day. But instead, he answered: "No. No, it's not practical."

Aahna nodded. The two sat on the bench together, as they had done a dozen times before, and remained in silence.

"What happened to your hand?" Daniel asked, finally noticing the bandages and wanting to break the silence.

"I cut my hand on a glass statue."

"Does it hurt?"

"Compared to what?" Aahna replied.

Daniel closed his eyes. "I have to get back to the office," he said, realizing that this would have to be their goodbye.

Aahna, most likely realizing the same thing, put her head in her hands. "How did this get so complicated?"

"These things are always complicated. That's what makes them memorable I suppose."

Daniel stood up from the bench. Aahna joined him a moment later and the two stood facing each other.

"I don't want you to ever believe that I'm abandoning you," he started. "I want you to know that this has been the best few months of my life, and that is only because of you."

The tears started to fall down Aahna's face.

"You are everything that I will remember about this country," he continued. "And you are the strongest person I know."

"Yet I don't have the strength to walk away from you," she said, resting her forehead against his chest.

He placed his chin on her head. "I hope that your family forgives you for everything. And that one day, you find the happiness you deserve."

Aahna tears came even faster now. She pulled herself away from his chest and looked into his eyes.

Daniel glanced away from her, his heart searing with pain. It was now or never. He whispered in her ear, "Know that three thousand miles away, there will always be someone who is thinking of you. Goodbye, Aahna." He kissed her firmly on the forehead, and then pulled himself away. Not able to look at her again, he turned around and headed back to the office building. He could only hope that the sounds he heard behind him were from a small animal whimpering, and not of a girl crying from a broken heart.

***

The airport was hot and muggy. Passengers sitting at the gate filled the large armchairs row by row, column by column. The Harp clan had managed to find three seats together, with Daniel and Paul stretched out and Megan wandering around taking pictures of large, framed shots of famous landmarks.

"Is she really taking pictures of pictures?" Daniel asked Paul.

"Only of the places we didn't visit on the trip."

Daniel rolled his eyes. His mood had been off during the entire tour. He had tried to forget about Aahna over the last ten days but every sculpture or garden had reminded him of their relationship.

Paul and Megan had given up trying to distract him, and instead embarked on day-long journeys through deserts and temples, while Daniel roamed the streets alone and miserable. He stayed away from common attractions, filled with happy families and curious foreigners. He found himself drawn to small shops filled with locals, immersing himself in the confusion of their language. His struggle to understand the words hurt his brain, but it was a much needed distraction from all the other thoughts swarming around. He had made an exception for one attraction, the Taj Mahal. The long standing tribute to true love was a sight he had wanted to see and experience for many years.

The story behind the exquisite landmark was even more captivating. A king, mourning the loss of his great love had erected the giant tomb in her honor. Forced out of power by his greedy son, he spent the last few years of his life locked up in a tiny room, with only the tomb as his view. It had long since become a symbol of eternal love. Ironic, Daniel had thought, that a country with such restrictions on marriage and romance, could produce one of the most famous love stories of all time.

Having seen other attractions with Aahna, Daniel longed for her insight on this particular landmark, and in that instant he realized how much he truly missed her. This had spun Daniel into an even further depression for the remainder of the trip.

"What time are we boarding again?" Megan asked, plopping herself next to Paul.

"Should be soon," Daniel replied.

"You must miss home no? It's been so long," Megan said.

"I've had distractions," Daniel replied testily.

Megan, taking that as her hint to stay quiet, got up and headed to the gift shop.

"She couldn't make it to the airport?" Paul asked when his fiancée was out of earshot.

"I told her not to come," Daniel replied.

Paul leaned forward slightly, resting his elbows on his knees. "But you were secretly hoping she would be here weren't you?"

"For what? So that I could wave to her in a large crowd?"

"So that you could see her one last time."

Daniel stayed quiet, ignoring the truth that lay in front of him.

"Man, I saw how crappy you felt. This wasn't just some fling was it?"

"I don't know what it was."

Daniel stared at the attendant at the gate door, hoping the boarding would start soon. They were finally headed home. After nearly five months of a country that had shown him the highs and lows of mankind, Daniel was ready to step on the plane, and leave it all behind.

***

Aahna grasped on the railing, both of her fists clenched along the rusted, metal rod that was the only thing separating her from the tarmac below. Her long-time family friend Paresh, a baggage-handler at the airport stood guard at the bottom of the stairs. It was nearly one in the morning and airport security in these areas was relatively lax due to the small number of flights leaving at this time of night. Paresh had managed to wave her in through the employee's area and allowed her to head up the stairs that would give her a clear view of a particular plane. She didn't know how she had gotten up the nerve to sneak out of the house so late, but there she stood, assuming that no upcoming punishment from her family would be worse than the pain she felt in that moment.

In the distance, three Canadians walked on the tarmac towards a waiting airplane. A man and a woman walked in stride together, talking to each other and laughing occasionally. Following closely behind them, another man with the same hair and stature as the first, hoisted his shoulder bag from one arm to the other. A strong breeze came through, and he zipped up his light jacket, shoving his hands into his pockets.

Aahna stared at the man from the small perch where she stood. She knew she only had a few minutes before an airport employee realized she shouldn't be standing there. Down below Paresh coughed, a signal that she should hurry up and say goodbye.

Goodbye.

That was the whole reason she risked another blow-up with her family. Aahna watched as Daniel looked down on the ground while he walked behind Paul and Megan. She was hoping maybe, just maybe he could sense that she was there. But he kept on walking, seemingly in a hurry to leave her homeland.

Aahna breathed out slowly. There were no tears in her eyes as this gentle man started to ascend the stairs onto the plane. A smile formed on her lips, remembering the first time she saw him at his desk. At that time she had run away when he glanced up at her. Now she would give anything for him to look in her direction. Aahna looked down at her hands, the same ones he had held so many times. When she looked up again, he was gone.

***

I can't believe I didn't get to see her one last time, Daniel thought to himself, as he stared out the window of the plane.

***

I cannot believe I saw him one last time, Aahna thought as she finally descended her perch and headed home.

Chapter Eight

Six Months Later

The flight from San Francisco back to Toronto had been long. Although it was a direct flight, Daniel had booked his ticket late and ended up in a middle seat between a man who couldn't stop coughing, and a woman who couldn't stop talking. She had wanted to know everything about Daniel, if only to have him then politely ask about her life.

He had wanted nothing more than to sleep on the plane, perhaps catch a quick movie and just relax in general. The business trip with the team in San Francisco had been fun, with a reason to go drinking almost every night. But the three hour time difference and the all-day meetings had left Daniel exhausted, and aching for his own bed.

As the flight touched down back in Toronto, Daniel de-planed as quickly as possible with the hopes of losing his seatmates once and for all. He jetted through the customs line and headed down the escalators to wait for his baggage.

Hundreds of fellow passengers from different flights thronged the baggage claim area, each one looking for their carousel. He pushed his way through the crowd and headed towards carousel nine, keeping his head down and hoping not to run into the talkative and nosy woman from the plane. The carousel had already started spinning by the time Daniel arrived and he anxiously awaited for his navy blue suitcase. Nearby, a young woman stood talking on her cell phone. Daniel couldn't see her face, and didn't recognize her from the plane, but there was something familiar about her. She had short black hair in a stylized cut, and wore a black blouse with fitted gray business skirt. Her heels elevated her somewhat, but Daniel could tell she was considerably shorter than the people standing around her. When she didn't look up, he moved his eyes away from her and continued to scan for his luggage.

As his suitcase found its way from the entrance belt to the part of the carousel nearest to him, Daniel leaned forward, prepared to heave his suitcase at the exact right moment. The suitcase neared him and he grabbed the top handle. At the same instance, the woman on her cell phone burst out laughing. It wasn't the suddenness of the laughter, or the volume of it that caused Daniel to lose his grip and almost fall backwards. It was once again, the familiarity of her. The bag continued past Daniel on the carousel, but he didn't care. He found himself walking towards this woman now. She burst out laughing again and it caused him to stop in his tracks. It had been over six months since he had heard that sound. An infectious and clearly distinctive giggle, it was a sound that still haunted him.

Before he could even stop himself, Daniel found his hand reaching out and pulling on the arm of the stranger with the phone. As if in slow motion, the woman turned around, clearly annoyed by this sudden disruption. It was all Daniel could do to not gasp.

Her hair was different, and her clothes were from the Western world, but everything else was the same. Her eyes were large, expressive and dark brown, her nose slanted slightly to the right, sitting just above a small mouth with full lips. Her body was petite, her arms slender but toned and her complexion was on the darker side of cocoa.

Ignoring the surroundings and the cosmetics, Daniel knew he was staring into the eyes of his beloved Aahna.

"Can I help you?" the woman said abruptly. Apparently not impressed with having her phone call disrupted by a complete stranger, she pulled her arm away and stepped back slightly.

Her voice left no sign of an accent, her tone and attitude similar to all the other Canadian women in his life. Daniel, still unable to come to terms with what was happening, remained speechless.

"Creep," she muttered, turning around and walking to the other side of the baggage carousel.

"Excuse me," a man said. "You're blocking the luggage."

Daniel moved away from the carousel stunned from the exchange a few seconds prior. He ignored his suitcase as it took another turn on the belt and went to find a place to sit. Scratching his head, he contemplated all the possible scenarios. Had Aahna found a way to come to Canada, and change her entire lifestyle to be with him as a surprise? Unlikely. Had that been the case, she wouldn't have flat out ignored him.

This woman had no idea who he was, but there she stood, in the exact shell as Aahna, but visibly having lived a different life entirely. Daniel's head continued to spin and he rubbed his eyes and face roughly. From a distance, he spotted her again. She had retrieved her bags and was headed out towards the exit. Daniel wanted to run after her, if only to explain himself. Worried, that she would completely freak out this time, causing airport officers of every rank to pounce on him, Daniel restrained himself and stayed glued to his seat until she exited the baggage claim gate.

He sighed, chalking everything up to an illusion, and potentially realizing that perhaps she didn't look *exactly* like Aahna. But rather, she had similar features, and they had triggered a deep-seeded feeling in him that had been suppressed for the last six months. As he walked over to retrieve his bag, which was now on its fifth and lonelier cycle around the carousel, he thought about all of the emotions he had suffered through.

In the first month back, his emotions had ranged from sadness to emptiness to outright grief and anger. The emptiness wasn't just due to Aahna. He had missed his new life in Kolkata, and all of the sights and sounds that he had experienced day in and day out. Even his bustling downtown condo in Toronto couldn't compare to the wonderful chaos of a city he had grown to love. His boss had been right about the people and the culture. But in that same month, he felt Aahna's presence everywhere. Daniel still exchanged emails regularly with Sunil, but it took all he had to not ask about her. Sunil had made his feelings clear about their relationship the moment he had decided to put Daniel back on a plane, irrespective of his work commitments. Daniel had not wanted to bring up anything that might further sour their work relationship.

Even at the office, Daniel felt a ping of sadness when he saw the cleaning staff come in to start dusting and taking out the garbage.

Paul and Megan had finalized their wedding date, and as the obvious choice for best man, Daniel had done his best to throw himself into their wedding preparations. From planning the bachelor party, to attending food and wine tastings for the dinner menu, Daniel provided his full support as the couple looked forward to their big day, a mere two months away now.

After the third month, Daniel had finally started to feel normal. He couldn't pinpoint the exact date and time, but the loneliness had slowly started to subside. He went to work in a more jovial mood, and even allowed himself to be setup on a few dates. There were no life partners in the mix, but the ladies were certainly pretty enough for a much needed temporary distraction. His life had finally reached regularity, but now his world had come full circle as he stood once again in an airport, devastated over a girl.

***

The car took longer than normal to start up as Daniel sat behind the driver's seat. Having not driven it in four days in the winter months took a toll on his old sedan. Having never been one for cars, Daniel had been driving the same vehicle for nearly eight years. The car was paid off, one less debt he owed to a bank and he wanted to keep it that way for as long as possible.

It was Sunday afternoon, which meant it was time for another bi-weekly visit to his parent's house. Megan and Paul would be arriving later, visiting a bakery first for their wedding cake tasting and therefore leaving him alone with his parents. Trips to St. Catherines always included the entire family, and if there were any reasons for solo visits, they were a result of the execution of administrative tasks only. If the parents visited the Harp brothers in the city, the trip constituted of museum tours or walks in a park. Daniel hadn't sat by himself and had a conversation with just his parents in quite some time.

After his arrival back to Canada six months prior, his parents had welcomed him with open arms, although he knew his mother was simply relieved he hadn't contracted anything while he was away. Richard was his usual stern self, but he seemed pleased that Daniel had returned in one piece and was now focused on North American travels primarily.

The drive to St. Catherines took longer than normal. Snow had begun to fall even though it was only late October. That wasn't uncommon entirely, but snow for people who hadn't gotten their winter tires yet always resulted in an adventure on the highways.

Daniel drove slowly, using the time in the car to ponder the strange incident in the airport two days ago. He was certain that the girl he met looked exactly like Aahna. He wasn't just imagining the resemblance. He wished Paul or Megan was with him, if only to prove he wasn't slowly losing his mind. He hadn't even gotten her name, meaning he had absolutely no way of tracking her down again. She had come into his life in order to vanish. Kind of like Aahna, he thought ironically.

Daniel hoped that the evening with his parents wouldn't result in more setups. Now that he was back and inevitably single, his mother had taken it upon herself to introduce him to the most random of girls. Some were nice; daughters of her friends. Daniel could sense the desperation in others though, as if the biological clock inside of them required a man to commit to marriage four dates in. Still unsure about his readiness for a commitment, Daniel stayed away from these women as much as possible. He recalled one date where he simply chugged down a cup of hot coffee in order to pay the bill and leave in a hurry. Regardless, this year was his brother's year. And he was happy to do his part as the best man. If only his mother could promise no 'arranged meetings' at the wedding.

Pulling into the family home, he headed up the driveway. The snow was falling harder in this part of town and he hiked the collar up on his jacket as he walked to the front door. The plants were slowly getting buried under the snow, and the flakes had taken over the branches on the trees. He couldn't remember the last time his cozy house had looked like a picture postcard.

After exchanging pleasantries, Daniel took his usual seat on the couch near the TV and Richard and Sophia arranged themselves across from him on the plush, tan colored couch. It was quiet for the first few moments, everyone clearly missing Paul's knack for small talk.

"How was San Francisco?" his mother started.

"It was good. They're going to send me back there again next week." Daniel shifted himself on the couch.

"Again?" Richard asked.

"They want me to head a project there, so it's going to take a few more weeks. I'll probably be going quite a bit in the next months."

"Well of all the places you could travel, San Francisco is quite lovely," his mother responded.

Ignoring the veiled dig about his previous trip, Daniel started munching on the chips that were placed in the bowl in front of him.

"Will you be bringing a date to the wedding?" Richard asked, bluntly.

Daniel looked up in surprise. Of all the questions his father could ask him, he was in awe that this was on his radar.

Sophia smiled at her son, clearly wanting to know the answer as well.

"I'm not sure yet," Daniel responded vaguely.

"Don't Paul and Megan need an RSVP soon?" Sophia asked politely.

Daniel's eyes squinted toward his parents. This was certainly a conversation he wasn't expecting. "Yes, in two weeks. I'll give *Paul and Megan* my answer then." His tone was final.

The three members of the Harp family looked at their watches at the same time, willing the missing members to arrive at any moment.

As if on cue, the front door swung open and Paul and Megan burst in.

"Wow, it's really coming down out there," Paul exclaimed, brushing snow off his jacket and stomping his feet on the welcome mat. Richard and Sophia jumped up from the couch to welcome their son and future daughter-in-law, leaving Daniel on the couch. Daniel sneaked a glance at his phone, hoping some urgent email had come through about work, but no such luck.

"How was the bakery?" Sophia inquired as the foursome headed back into the living room.

"It was lovely!" Megan exclaimed, giving Daniel a quick hug as she sat down next to him. "The samples were delicious."

"Delicious, yes," Paul said nodding at his brother. "But not worth twelve hundred dollars."

"Twelve hundred dollars for a cake," Richard retorted. "What exactly is it made out of?"

"Cakes are like art now," Megan said. "You have to pay for quality."

"It's a wedding," Paul said. "Not a funeral."

"You would pay twelve hundred dollars for a cake at a funeral?" Megan raised her eyebrow.

"I mean, it's not the last thing we're going to be spending money on. And there are tons of other things we still haven't purchased yet."

"I said I would go cheaper on the centerpieces and favors!" Megan protested. "Flea markets and what not."

"Oh you can get such lovely items there now," Sophia chimed in.

Paul threw his head back on the loveseat, clearly frustrated with this repeated conversation.

"Let's get a drink in the kitchen, boys," Richard said, already halfway up from the couch. Daniel and Paul followed their father. Richard grabbed beers out of the fridge and passed them around. After taking a swig, Richard said: "So Daniel's not sure if he's bringing a date to your wedding."

"Jesus," Daniel exclaimed. "Is there nothing else three grown men can talk about?"

Paul laughed. "Well you have two more weeks to decide. Personally I don't care, although if I was single I wouldn't want to bring some random chic to a wedding. There should be plenty of desperate, lonely girls to hook up with." Paul winked at his brother.

Richard rolled his eyes, with Daniel following suit.

"Your mom tells me that Betsy Jones' daughter recently moved out of her boyfriend's place. She'll be at the wedding." Richard took another swig of the beer.

"I have the feeling that Daniel's tastes have changed to more, um, exotic women."

Daniel glared at his younger brother. He had sworn Paul to secrecy about his relationship. Now that Aahna and Daniel were apart, there was no reason to explain the drama to his parents. They wouldn't understand, and his father would of course assume it was a ploy for Aahna to come to Canada and leave him at her earliest convenience. There were a million conversations he was more than happy to dodge.

"What does your brother mean by that?" Richard asked.

"Nothing," Daniel replied before Paul could answer. "I think he's drunk."

"I've had half a beer," Paul said.

"You've always been a lightweight," Daniel said, finishing off his beer and getting up from the kitchen table. "I'm going to go discuss flowers now if you don't mind. That conversation seems far more interesting than where this one is headed."

Daniel left the kitchen, leaving a bewildered father and an amused brother behind. As he made his way back to the living room, he could hear the trails of his mother's voice.

"...once saw a gorgeous candle sitting on one of those mirrored plates..."

From the kitchen, Daniel heard his brother speak up.

"He'll be fine. He's just enjoying the bachelor life now."

"Seems like he's been enjoying it for quite some time," Richard replied.

Daniel stood in the foyer between the kitchen and the living room, feeling isolated from his own family in that moment. He had no desire to return to either room, and so he perched himself on the stairs. Pulling his phone out, he began to sift through unread work emails. Right now, it was the only part of this life that didn't disappoint him.

Chapter Nine

"Boarding pass please," the airport attendant said.

Anita fished her boarding pass out of the back of her pocket and handed it to the attendant.

"The line-up for your flight hasn't started yet. Please sit in this lobby and we will make an announcement when you can get in line."

Anita nodded and headed inside the make-shift lobby. Having been travelling almost weekly for the last three months she was used to the airport process. She shoved the boarding pass into her purse, and juggling her laptop bag and carry-on she headed to an empty chair facing a window that overlooked an empty tarmac.

Plopping herself down, she arranged all of her belongings. She counted the number of trips she still had to take before she could finally fly elite status. More importantly, before she could sit in a lounge and have a drink prior to boarding her flight. Not that she needed to drink at eight in the morning. But it was certainly nice to have that option.

Anita closed her eyes for a few moments, the early Monday morning rising finally catching up to her. The trip to Chicago would take just over an hour, but the production of flying resulted in almost four hours of wasted time door to door. Being forced to drive straight to the office before even heading to the hotel was another annoyance that Anita wasn't looking forward to.

Oh well, she thought to herself. The client visits were going well and Anita had been promised a promotion as soon as the project was over. Her generic title as 'Consultant' would finally have a 'Senior' in front of it, and that was all she needed to make her happy at this time.

Sure, a boyfriend would be nice. But that too would come in due time. Having just gotten out of a three year relationship did leave her slightly lonely. And working with men who switched from talking about hockey to complaining about how their girlfriends didn't let them watch hockey was also getting tiresome. But she had embraced her newfound single status by taking up a course in painting, hanging out with more of her friends, and spending time with her adorable nephew and niece. If she kept herself busy, then coming home to an empty condo didn't seem too rough.

Anita opened her eyes when the sun suddenly peaked out from behind the clouds and aimed their rays directly at her. It felt nice for only a second, before the blinding light became too much to bear.

Sighing, she gathered all of her belongings again and headed to the opposite end of the waiting area, away from the windows. This area was fuller, so she wandered up and down two aisles before finding an empty seat. Trying to avoid hitting anyone, Anita settled into the empty seat, re-organizing her bags on the floor in front of her. She fished her book out of her purse, realizing the stark contrast between her worn down paperback and the shiny tablets everyone else was holding.

Anita was careful that day to dress in her business suit. Having a petite frame and young looking face, most fellow passengers mistook her for a university student traveling alone. Some mistook her as being even younger. She remembered the time an elderly couple sitting next to her bought her lunch on the plane thinking it was probably her first flight travelling by herself. She graciously accepted, all the while thinking how she could have expensed all three of their meals. Anita giggled to herself, recalling the memory.

Having not opened her book yet, she put it back in her purse and instead chose to people watch. The majority of travelers were on business, like her. Their heads were buried into their phones, tablets or laptops, as they furiously tried to get in as much work as possible before they were cut off while sitting in the sky. A few families also lingered nearby. Their attire of beach clothes implied they were leaving the cold winter of Toronto for a tropical destination. Anita envied them for a moment, having not taken a vacation in almost a year. Well she had visited India the year before with her parents, but she never really counted that as a vacation. Visiting relatives and watching them watch television was not the most effective use of her time. But still, she had been making those trips for years, and they were as much a part of her as anything else in her life.

Anita's eyes wandered to a young mother playing with small child. The mother looked no older than Anita, but the child was at least three or four. Anita couldn't imagine having a child of that age at this point in her life, but she knew she wanted kids one day. At least two; a boy and a girl. A common, simple dream, she thought.

"Yes sir, your flight will be called soon."

Anita looked up as the same airport attendant directed a man to the waiting area. He was over six feet tall, had dusty blond hair and bright blue eyes. His checkered blue shirt was tucked neatly into gray pants, and the black belt and shoes finished off the ensemble. He shifted his laptop bag from his right shoulder to his left as he pulled his carry-on behind him. Anita squinted as he walked through the waiting area. He looked vaguely familiar.

She continued to stare at him as he looked for an empty seat. Circling back, the man made his way from the windows over to the area where Anita was sitting. She kept her gaze focused on him, wondering how she knew him. In that instant, the man caught Anita staring.

She lowered her eyes reflexively, but just as quickly raised them back, still intrigued by the familiarity of this good looking man.

He had stopped in his tracks and his gaze was focused right at her. The look was so intense Anita almost turned around, wondering if he was looking at someone else. His mouth was slightly open, as if in disbelief, and he looked to be pondering his next move.

That's weird, Anita thought. He almost looks like he recognizes me too.

He tilted his head sideways, and in that second the memory clicked for Anita. Last Friday. Anita lowered her head again. It was the crazy guy that had started talking to her while she was on the phone. Oh great. Figures I would run into the crazy guys again, she thought to herself. She looked up slowly, to see if he had moved. He had, but only closer to her. There were no seats near her that were empty, thank goodness, but he still kept walking closer.

Anita glanced around at her surroundings, wondering which person would come to her aid when she started screaming. She shifted in her seat as he walked right up to her. Once in front of her, he knelt down, as if he didn't want to appear intimidating.

Because of their height difference, the kneeling resulted in Anita meeting her admirer's gaze straight on.

"I don't want to scare you," the man started quietly.

Anita noticed her seat neighbor look up from the mobile device he was holding. He glanced at both of them with a curious look on his face. She didn't blame him.

"You just look like someone I know really well," the man continued.

Anita wasn't sure if she should respond and encourage this conversation to continue. But there was a gentleness in his extraordinarily pretty eyes. He smiled slightly, and Anita wondered if having a hot stalker was a story she could tell her friends later.

"I don't mean you just look like her. I mean you look identical to her. So much so that I'm having a hard time believing you're actually someone else."

Am I getting hit on in an airport? Anita thought, realizing this sounded like some weird pickup line. Her neighbor must have thought the same thing because he rolled his eyes and went back to scrolling on his phone.

"Maybe you and I have met before," Anita finally said as she tried to figure out where this was leading. God he's gorgeous, she thought again, suddenly realizing that if he was even remotely unattractive she would have called airport security already. She opted to ignore her own shallowness for the moment.

"No, you see, the girl you resemble lives in India."

Anita gave him a puzzled expression. This wasn't a line. He was actually mistaking her for someone else. Damn.

She sighed. "I've been there many times so perhaps you saw me there. Although it's unlikely, since there are about one billion other people you could have run into."

"It's just uncanny," the man continued.

Anita started to get as bored as the man sitting next to her. "Okay, well, I don't know what to tell you. Is there anything else you need?" She felt bad speaking rudely to someone who was so attractive. But since he didn't appear to actually be interested in her, she forgave herself.

"Your name?" he said.

Is this guy for real? She thought. "I'm not telling you that, I don't even know you."

"I just need to know for sure."

"Dude, seriously, this is the work pick up I've ever seen," the neighbor blurt out.

The man ignored the comment. "You don't know anyone named Aahna do you?"

He said the name softly, as if it caused him pain. Anita saw the gentleness again, and felt sorry for him for some reason. He sounded like he really cared about this girl.

"No," she responded. "I don't, I'm sorry."

His eyes appeared sad, and the corners of his mouth turned downward. He looked around, as if he wasn't sure what to do next.

Anita suddenly realized how embarrassed he must feel, and what courage it must have taken him to walk up to a perfect stranger at an airport, only to engage in an even stranger conversation.

"I really am sorry," Anita repeated. "Was she your girlfriend?"

"Oh my God, is this actually working?" The neighbor grabbed his bags and got up. "Take my seat, buddy. You deserve a medal if this works." He strode off not looking back.

The man sat down next to Anita. "You could say that, but she was more than just a girlfriend."

"She definitely sounds important to you. I'm sorry I couldn't be of more help."

"I don't really know what I expected when I came up to you."

Anita looked away from his intense gaze. "We all do crazy things when we're in love."

The man laughed. It was a sweet laugh. "I'm sorry for bothering you."

Their eyes locked again and Anita felt the first signs of a butterfly in her stomach. She pushed the feeling down, since this man all but admitted he was head over heels for someone else.

"Honestly don't worry about it. I didn't mean to be rude earlier," she paused. "I'm Anita."

The man's perfectly white teeth and thin lips formed into a beautiful smile. "It's nice to meet you, Anita. I'm Daniel. Daniel Harp."

***

"So you met a guy at the airport who thought you were someone else, and not only did he emphasize that he had feelings for this other person, he somehow managed to get you to ask him out?"

Anita took another sip of her white wine as her best friend and current heckler, Janette, retold the now infamous story.

"I didn't ask him out. I merely asked if he wants to have coffee."

"That's what 'asking out' means," Janette emphasized. "Of all the people to be swayed by a pick-up line, I am honestly surprised."

"It wasn't like that. You had to be there. There was something in his eyes that exuded truth."

"He sounds like a flake," Janette responded curtly.

Anita gave her friend a look.

"Oh c'mon, if I told you this story, you would have re-enacted the scene countless times by now!"

Anita couldn't argue with her. "I'm not saying it wasn't a line. It just happened to be an effective one."

"Clearly."

"You should have seen the way he looked. If you were in my shoes, you would have dragged him onto your flight and asked him to join the mile high club."

"Maybe, but you're not me. You're Ms. Sensible!"

Anita sighed. That part was true. But maybe she was tired of being the responsible, well-mannered, always-make-the-right-decision girl. Her friends were allowed to get up to nonsense without being judged, why couldn't she? She sipped her white wine thoughtfully.

The bar was louder than on most nights. It had been Anita and Janette's long-time hangout since they both started working downtown together. The majority of their co-workers from the bank also made an appearance after work, after putting in a stressful ten or eleven hour day, the new norm in the 21st century. Anita loved her job at the bank, having been there since she graduated university ten years prior. Most of her friends had switched jobs several times since then but she was planning on becoming a lifer. Her boss was fantastic and personable, and the work remained challenging. Sure there were good and bad days, but they were nothing compared to the horror stories she had heard from other people. Janette had joined the company only two weeks after Anita and the two had become fast friends. Even after Janette had switched departments and moved to an office down the street, the pair met up as often as they could. Having always been single around the same time also allowed for that.

"He lives around here," Anita said, waving down the bartender for another wine.

"Well, I hope he's a good guy for your sake. You've been going out with some real losers lately."

"They haven't been losers per se."

"Really?" Janette pressed. "What would you call a guy that stops by a random house during your date to *pick up his stash?*"

"Efficient."

Janette raised an eyebrow.

"All right, all right, so they haven't been anyone to email home about," Anita said.

"I'm glad you agree." Janette finished the last of her rye and ginger and began picking at the plate of calamari that sat between them. "Speaking of home, how are the folks?"

"They're fine. Arguing as usual, but nothing new or dramatic."

"I don't really get how your parents can fight all the time."

"What do you expect? They had an arranged marriage. In some cases, it works. In other cases, well you have my parents."

"Are they still bugging you to get married?"

"My mom is, obviously. My dad's just happy that I have a good job and own property." Anita grabbed a forkful of squid and popped it into her mouth. Calamari had been her weakness for as long as she could remember, ordering it as an appetizer at nearly every restaurant she frequented.

"What age does your mom think you should get married?"

"Hmm, I don't know. The age I am right after I land the right job?"

"So, ten years ago then."

"You got it."

Janette laughed. "I wish my parents had as much vested interest in me as your parents do."

"No you don't," Anita replied. "Especially when you realize that the majority of my mom's concerns are around what her friends will think of an unmarried woman of my age living alone somewhere." Anita chuckled to herself. Her mother was dear to her. Both of her parents were. And while she recognized that quite a few personality traits from both of them were embedded squarely in her, she knew their largest differences was due to how contrarily they had been raised. They had been brought up believing in arranged marriages, and a woman's key role in a man's life. Thirty-five years of living in a foreign land had changed the mind of her father who had embraced modernity as quickly as possible. However, her mother held firmly to her beliefs. Anita knew her mother had no real interest in arranging a marriage for her only child, she merely wanted to see her happy. However, in her mother's mind, happiness implied marriage and kids, and everything before that were just the preliminary tests leading up to the final exam. If Anita could just land the husband, she could finally produce the grandchildren which she knew her mother was aching for.

Her luck with men had been abysmal lately, which is why she was slightly excited and intrigued by the handsome stranger she had met at the airport. She knew anything serious was unlikely. He was still obviously affected by someone else. Anita found it interesting that he had been to India and had met someone. She must be something special, Anita thought to herself. What random luck for this girl that she could catch the attention of this gorgeous Canadian man; while Anita had apparently lived down the street from him all this time yet only landed drug users and men who had commitment issues. Maybe her luck was slowly about to change.

"Wanna get going?" Janette asked.

Anita nodded and Janette flagged down the bartender for the bill.

"When is your date by the way?"

"Tuesday. We're meeting for drinks at the Front Street Winery," Anita replied, remembering how she was the one who had proposed not only the outing, but the date and location. Thinking back now, she wondered if Daniel had merely accepted the date in lieu of feeling bad after showing no interest in her directly. She pushed the thought out of her mind, reminding herself that she was a great catch and that a guy like Daniel would be lucky to go out with her.

Janette saddled up the bill and both girls grabbed their heavy winter coats and gloves.

Anita, maneuvering into her jacket while holding her gloves and purse precariously, only hoped that she could feel as confident on Tuesday as she was feeling today, and that maybe, just maybe, she could one day tell her grandkids a funny story, about the way she had met her soul mate.

***

The cold and wind were picking up even stronger as Anita made her way down Front Street. Her fancy gloves, while looking good, were neither warm nor water-resistant for the slight snow that had started to fall. She refused to wear a hat and ruin her hair, so instead she shoved her face as far into a scarf as she could without ruining her makeup.

It had taken her nearly an hour to figure out what to wear. Anita was normally never this vain or indecisive, but something about this particular date made her linger in front of her mirror for far too long. In the end she had chosen a blue patterned, chiffon top with attached scarf, and black pants with black high heeled boots. The top was sleeveless, so she opted for her simple black fitted cardigan to wear on top.

Now, as she trudged through the downtown core, Anita was cursing the high-heeled boots as she found herself slipping on every uneven part of the sidewalk. This guy better be worth it, she thought. Ironically, the fifteen minute walk from her apartment to the venue resulted in passing other infamous landmarks from previous dates. The pharmacy that she had run to when her stockings had a tear and she was already late for a party with a corporate lawyer. The coffee shop where she met with the sculptor Janette had set her up with, coffee being the only drink the unemployed aspiring artist could afford. The Italian bistro with the comedic doctor who spent the entire evening mocking people in the restaurant or dropping one-liners constantly, without any thought to a real conversation. It was like witnessing a slideshow of her dating life, the only thing missing was the slightly uplifting song in the background. As she rounded the last corner, Anita stood face to face with the venue of her latest potential conquest. She breezed past the small lineup that was beginning to form and headed inside, pushing past the last few people that were blocking the door.

The bar was already crowded, with people waiting for tables and meeting friends. Hugs and handshakes were exchanged by the second as Anita slowly maneuvered her way over to the hostess. In her early twenties and wearing a short black dress, designed solely to make men drool and for women to feel even worse about themselves, the hostess ignored Anita as she took reservations on the phone. Her tone was arrogant, as if she and only she held the key to everyone's happiness that evening.

After hanging up the phone, the hostess spent another two minutes jotting down notes and names on a schedule so complicated that even Anita, with her math degree, was nonplussed. Finally, the hostess looked up and appeared to notice Anita for the first time.

"I was wondering how long the wait is to get a table for two for drinks," Anita shouted over the din.

"About forty-five minutes," the hostess responded, haughtily.

Ugh, Anita thought. Even on a Tuesday? "Okay, I'll wait thanks. My name's Anita," she said, motioning her head towards the schedule. After the hostess added her name, Anita headed back through the crowd to look for Daniel. He was tall, so it would be easy to spot him she assumed. He didn't look to be there yet, so she stood against a console and pretended to play with her phone, trying not to appear too desperate.

After only a few minutes of pretend surfing, Anita felt a tap on her shoulder. She came face-to-chest with a dark black jacket covered in snow that had already started to melt. Bright blue eyes twinkled as Daniel smiled down at her. "Sorry I'm late," he said.

The voice was intoxicating as Daniel leaned closer to her while people pushed their way past them. Anita secretly hoped that someone would knock Daniel right into her, much like what she'd seen in every romantic comedy.

He seemed taller than she recalled, most likely because he was standing right next to her now instead of crouching in front of her seat whilst professing his love for another girl. Glad that she chose to wear her heels and gain the additional three inches on her five foot stature, Anita smiled back at him.

"Apparently the wait is going to be forty-five minutes," Anita started. "Not sure if you wanted to wait that long or go somewhere else?"

"Hmm, that is a bit long," Daniel said.

Dang, he wants to make this a quick drink, Anita over-analyzed to herself.

"There's a coffee shop down the street. It's got some comfortable chairs and board games, you know in case we realize we have nothing in common." Daniel winked at Anita, and she could actually feel her knees begin to buckle.

The coffee shop was nestled in between a larger pharmacy chain and a small boutique of women's clothing. The walk was only a few minutes but Anita had a hard time keeping up with Daniel's long strides and the icy sidewalks. She debated holding on to his arm but realized it was a little early in the evening to start her coy flirting techniques. The ambience of the shop exuded warmth as soon as they stepped into the small venue. A fireplace crackled on one side, and there were wooden circular tables with patterned armchairs scattered everywhere. Most of the tables were taken up already with people holding steaming mugs and chatting with friends.

A spot in the corner was open and Daniel guided Anita through the darkened café to the back of the room where two chairs next to a big bookshelf of board games awaited them. A small table sat between the chairs with an antique lamp resting precariously. Anita plopped into the chair, if only to give her feet a break from her high heels. After giving their orders of hot chocolate and black coffee to the young waiter, Daniel and Anita rested back into their chairs to officially begin their date. Before Anita could say anything, Daniel started to speak.

"I wanted to apologize again about the mix-up at the airport. My head wasn't in the right place." He paused. "I was doing better, but seeing you kind of brought up some old feelings. I guess not what you want to hear on a first date."

Anita agreed to herself. "I'm not really sure how to respond to that. Did you want to talk about it?" Please don't, she thought.

Daniel shook his head. "No, no. I just really wanted to say that piece. Let's forget about it. Please, tell me about yourself." He smiled his brilliant smile causing Anita to forgive and forget in a heartbeat.

She adjusted her seat closer to the table and regaled the story of her life to the handsome man sitting across from her. He appeared to listen intently as she spoke about her parents and their dreams for her, about her relatively ordinary upbringing and her current job status. He asked relevant questions and encouraged Anita to continue speaking. She was comfortable with him and hadn't had an open conversation about her life with anyone other than her closest friends in quite some time.

When it was Daniel's turn to talk, he told a similar story about his childhood, parents, university and job. As Anita listened, she realized the story sounded almost scripted. Not false, but with the air of having been told many, many times. It made Anita a little self-conscious to suddenly realize how many dates a man like Daniel had potentially been on. To him, this could merely be another evening with just another girl, albeit one who looked remarkably similar to a past love.

Anita nodded at the right times and laughed at the right times, as she herself had been on enough dates in her life to distinguish those who were genuinely interested, and those who were merely passing the time. When it came time to discuss his trip to India, Anita noticed slight hesitation from Daniel. "What kind of places did you visit?" Anita asked, hoping to keep the conversation away from any sensitive territory.

Daniel appeared to relax slightly. "I think I visited pretty much every major landmark. I was such a tourist. But to be honest, the Victoria Memorial was still one of the most impressive."

"I thought so too," Anita agreed. "Did your Indian co-worker take you there?" As soon as the words left her mouth, the atmosphere between them changed.

Daniel shifted in his seat and took a sip of his coffee. He looked everywhere but at Anita.

"You went with her," Anita said softly, less a question and more a statement.

"Yeah," Daniel responded, equally softly.

"Sorry, I didn't mean to bring it up. I shouldn't have asked."

"It's fine. I don't know why I get like this. Sometimes I feel like a sappy thirteen-year old girl whose upset because her crush didn't ask her to the prom."

"Um, I don't think thirteen-year olds go to the prom, but I get what you're saying."

Daniel laughed. "I don't mean to be such a downer. You have nothing to do with this."

"I guess I'm sorry I look like her."

"I'm not," Daniel smiled and Anita found herself blushing.

An hour later they both decided to call it a night. Anita bundled up in her warm jacket and scarf and prepared to head down the wintery downtown street and back to her cozy apartment.

"Let me have the cab drop you off down the street," Daniel insisted. When she refused, Daniel offered to walk her back to her condo lobby and catch a cab from there.

As they headed into the cold, Anita looked up at him, processing the date in her mind. It was so-so she thought, but better than most first dates. No awkward moments, except for the giant elephant in the room known as the person who looked just like her. He can get over that, she thought to herself. And I can help him. With that final thought, she hopped over a patch of ice on the sidewalk, and then looped her arm in his as they walked into the wind.

Chapter Ten

Dearest Daniel,

It has been more than six months since you left my country and my life, and each day seems to crawl slower than the last. I watched as you got on the plane and never looked back. How can I expect you to? You have a life that is awaiting you. This trip was only a chapter in the story of your life. But in my story, it was the beginning, middle and the end.

My days have stayed the same since your departure. I still work for Sunil Sir and his family in their apartment. And since you are no longer in the country, my family has allowed me to continue working in Sunil Sir's office.

Every day is a challenge. In every second, I am consumed by thoughts of you. I picture your face clearly and I recall different memories of our time together.

The nights are even harder. I close my eyes and am left alone in silence. It is hard to imagine being entirely taken over by one single concept, but I have learned it is completely possible. I await the day when I can wake up and have such a fulfilling life that the thought of you is no longer attached to every breath I take.

My mother has become ill in the last few months. Her cough has gotten more serious, and Sunil Sir has helped us find a good doctor, but medicine will only work for so long. It is expensive, and my mother is having a hard time finding the strength to continue fighting. I fear that my actions have caused her to lose any hope in my future and it is this loss that is weakening her daily.

Sourav is doing better. His initial anger at our relationship has since calmed down, and we have been able to go back to the way things were. He believes he can take over the rickshaw business as his boss is retiring soon. As well, there is a girl in our neighborhood that is showing some interest, and provided my mother's strength returns soon, I foresee a wedding any day now. I can only hope that his life continues to grow and that it returns some of the joy into my mother's soul.

Raina and I have continued our friendship. I cannot stay mad at her. Her misfortune with a vicious husband is a far greater trial than anything I can ever truly understand. And to blame the weak for an outcome that was inevitable anyways makes no sense.

The weather has gotten cooler in our part of the world. I am sure it is not as cold your country, but for us, shawls and scarves have started to appear. The mornings are the hardest, and our tiny family spends most of the time huddled near a small fire on the stove.

I overheard my mother speaking to Sourav about potentially arranging a marriage for me. They want to look in another part of town for a boy, where any rumors of my relationship with you may not have reached. If you can count on anything in our people, it is gossip. I don't know how I feel about marrying someone. If he is kind and respectful to me, I know I should be grateful as things can be much worse.

If he is neither kind nor respectful, I hope I have the courage to run away. I don't know where I would go, but I feel that living life alone is better than an unhappy fate with someone else.

I have thought a lot about fate recently. In my alone time I try and see what reason you were brought into my life. Maybe it was to experience a small glimmer of hope about what happiness could really be. But to have it taken away is a cruelty I never expected. I don't believe that it is better to have loved. This is a pain that I can live without, and I am not sure that any amount of prior happiness has made it worthwhile.

I am sure you spend your days with many different girls. Or perhaps, with one serious girl. I can only hope you find true happiness with someone who will spend her days realizing how lucky she truly is. You can shine a light into any girl's heart. Of that, I am sure.

This is the eighth letter I have written to you since you have left. And like the others, I will not send it. I don't even have your address, nor can I ever ask Sunil Sir for it. But even if I did, I write these thoughts only in an attempt to heal myself. It has not yet worked.

I am sure you have long since forgotten about the young Indian maid whose eyes you opened and whose heart you stole. I do not blame you. I hardly leave an impression with the person that sells us milk. How can I leave an impression with someone like you?

I remember how you used to say my name. I can still hear it. I never told you what my name means, nor did you ask. It means "to exist". Up until six months ago, I never thought much of it. Mostly because every day was the same as yesterday, and there was nothing to exist for.

You have changed all that. Regardless of whatever happens in my life or yours, know that I exist entirely for you, and in the dreams that keep me awake at night, you feel the same way about me. I sincerely hope that you are well, and please remember that thousands of miles away, there is someone who thinks of you always.

Yours, in this life and the

next,

Aahna

Chapter Eleven

Daniel threw his keys onto the kitchen counter as he walked into his apartment. He had just returned from his second date, dinner and a movie with Anita, and a headache was slowly starting to form in the back of his head. A similar ache was also taking shape in his stomach, but he couldn't quite pinpoint the foundation of it. Throwing his jacket on the back of a chair, he settled down into his couch and turned the television on. Flipping through channels, Daniel barely noticed the characters, colors and plotlines passing him by. After about fifteen minutes of mindless surfing, he turned it off and tossed the remote next to him.

Twiddling his thumbs and resting his head on the back of couch, Daniel tried to picture the date with Anita. It was pleasant enough. She was a nice girl, and they did in actuality have many things in common. But Daniel had found himself moving away as she inched closer to him in the movie theater. And he didn't know why. She was obviously very attractive, but something didn't feel right. Her obvious similarities to Aahna were disconcerting to him and he almost felt she was merely a shell of the vibrant yet gentle girl he had fallen in love with.

Daniel knew he wasn't being fair to Anita. In all respects she could be a fantastic companion to some other guy. Perhaps if he had even met her a year ago their lives could be completely different. But he had to play with the cards he was dealt. And while he knew one day he could move on with a girl, there was no way he could start a new life with someone who would inevitably remind him of a heartache he wasn't ready to re-experience.

The phone rang, pulling Daniel out of his self-imposed misery.

"So Megan wants a horse-drawn carriage to circle around High Park in the dead of winter prior to us arriving at the reception," Paul said as soon as Daniel answered the phone. "What are your thoughts on that?"

"I have no thoughts on that since I don't spend a large part of my life watching romantic comedies."

"I know right! I only agreed to a winter wedding with the caveat that I could run from the car to the venue without ever feeling cold."

"Winter weddings are nice," Daniel said distractingly. He arbitrarily picked up a magazine and began leafing through it, not really in the mood to discuss his brother's wedding.

"I know they can be. I just assumed the 'winter' part of it would consist of me watching snow fall from inside."

"It can still be that," Daniel said, his enthusiasm waning as the conversation continued.

"Anyway, what's happening with you? You sound distracted."

Daniel hesitated, wondering if he should tell Paul about Anita. He needed another perspective, and Paul was one of the few people in the world who knew about Aahna. He put the magazine down and went into the story of how he had run into Anita at the airport, leading all the way up to the date he just returned from. Daniel couldn't see Paul's expression but he pictured his brother's eyebrow rising higher and higher and his mouth dropping slowly as Daniel continued the story.

After Daniel finished, he paused, letting Paul process everything he had just told him.

"You managed to find a girl who looks exactly like Aahna over here in Canada?"

"Yes."

"And not only have you found her, she's actually interested in you and you've already been on a couple of dates?"

"Yes," Daniel repeated, contemplating flipping through the magazine again while Paul rehashed key parts of the conversation.

"Dude!" Paul exclaimed. "This is the greatest thing that could have ever happened to you!"

Daniel's ears perked up. "What are you talking about?" he said.

"I mean, this girl is the best of both worlds! No pun intended. Think about it, she's the girl you're in love with but she lives and works here. You can't make this stuff up!"

"Paul, you don't understand. She's not the same girl. I can't just lead her on if I don't truly have feelings for her."

"How can you not have feelings for her? You were so miserable when you got back from India, but here she is. This girl could save you!"

"It's not that easy. She looks like her. That's all. I can't just automatically fall for her."

"You've been on like what, two dates." Paul said. "Give it some time."

Daniel sighed. His brother didn't get it.

"Look," Paul said, appearing to understand the silence. "I know that this girl isn't going to be the same as Aahna. No girl will be. But eventually, you're going to have to get over her. So what's the harm in doing that with someone whom you should already be physically attracted to? Do you see what I mean?"

"Your theory makes sense on paper. But that's the only place it makes sense." Daniel got up from the couch and began pacing across his living room.

"Suit yourself. I am curious to meet this chic though," Paul said.

"I don't think that's happening. If I introduce you to her it means I'm planning to take this relationship further. And I'm not," Daniel said.

"What if I accidentally run into you guys somewhere?"

"Um, I don't think so."

Paul laughed. "It was worth a shot. Since you seem to have this figured out I'm going to bounce. I'll call you later in the week."

After Paul hung up, Daniel stared at the phone. He contemplated calling Anita, and telling her it was over. It was certainly going to have to be a phone conversation. Daniel had no desire to look her in the eyes and see Aahna's heartbreak all over again.

The headache that had started to form when he first came home was now encompassing his entire head. Daniel put on a pot of coffee, hoping to relieve the tension somehow. He looked at the phone again, when suddenly it rang.

Grabbing it on the third ring, Daniel answered.

"Hi, it's Anita," a voice said on the other side.

The headache started to pound. Daniel lifted his hand and squeezed the bridge of his nose between his eyes.

Anita continued. "I don't think what I'm about to say is going to come as a shock."

Daniel stayed quiet.

"I think we shouldn't see each other anymore," Anita said.

Daniel removed his hand from his face. What did she say?

"Hello?" Anita said.

"Sorry, I'm here. I'm just…processing."

"You're not surprised are you? I think you're a great guy, but your head seems to be elsewhere all the time. Probably with that girl from India."

Daniel knew he had to say something. She was giving him a way out and he felt grateful. "You're right. I was hoping it would go away, but seeing you makes it harder. I think you're great though!" he added quickly.

Anita laughed and Daniel felt relieved.

"Well no harm done," Anita said.

"I was actually going to call you and say the same thing. I mean, I could see if I felt differently after a couple more dates, but what's the point right? I don't want to lead you on."

"I appreciate it," Anita said.

They both paused and let the silence wash over them. Daniel wasn't sure what to say next.

"You must have really loved her," Anita finally said.

Daniel chose not to respond.

"Wow, I must really look like her to get you this upset," Anita chuckled to herself.

"It's uncanny, to be honest," Daniel said. "All the same features, the same height and build. If I didn't know any better, I would think you guys are twins or something."

This time Anita stayed quiet.

Ignoring the silence, Daniel rambled on. "But that's impossible, since you're born here."

"I never actually said I was born here, just that I grew up here."

A slow, eerie pang started to grow in Daniel's stomach. "Where were you born then?" he asked slowly.

"In India," Anita said quietly.

"Okay, but still, you have different parents." The coffee pot whistled signaling its completion. He ignored it, feeling he should give his full attention to this current conversation.

"Daniel, how much do I really look like her?" Anita asked in a strange voice.

"I told you," Daniel replied, his voice sounding equally strange. "Other than the clothes, hair and makeup, it's almost exact." He stared hard at a spot on the counter, not sure where else to look. "Anita, you do have different parents don't you?"

Silence.

"Please say something. What's going through your head right now?" Daniel pleaded. "Is there something you're not telling me?" Daniel could almost sense Anita closing her eyes on the other end.

"I was adopted," Anita finally said, her voice quavering. "From an orphanage in India, I was adopted."

***

The coffee pot hissed quietly as Daniel lifted the pot from the coffeemaker and slowly began pouring it in his favorite mug. His hand was shaking slightly and a few drops landed on the counter. The coffee did nothing to soothe his nerves as he waited impatiently for Anita to arrive. After she dropped the bombshell about her adoption, they both agreed they needed to meet in person immediately.

Daniel's head was swimming. The potential radical coincidence that he had landed on was looming over him. His earlier headache was gone, only to be replaced by a knot the size of a basketball resting uncomfortably in his stomach. Sitting still wasn't an option, but neither was pacing and drinking hot coffee. He abandoned the coffee in favor of using his pen as a drumstick against the counter to a random beat. When that got boring, he jumped off the counter and looked through the peephole in the door. Where was she? Was she putting makeup on or something?

He decided pacing was the only thing that could calm him down and so he began a brisk walk up and down the length of his kitchen to his living room. Every five rounds he checked his cell phone, to make sure it hadn't rung or that the battery was still charged.

The door knocked.

Before he could even answer it, Anita stormed into his living room. She was wearing no makeup and her hair was pulled back, the resemblance to Aahna even more striking. Daniel's breath caught in his throat.

"What the hell, Daniel?" Anita exclaimed, almost shouting. "Who are you?"

Daniel, startled by her reaction, stepped back slightly. In that second he realized the absolute bewilderment mixed with newfound knowledge that was probably cursing through Anita's veins. It was her life that was affected by this news. Her entire past that was being re-told. He was merely a bystander, a witness to events that were not going to change his life. The least he could do was let her react in a natural way.

"Anita, look, I understand this is all a little...," Daniel searched for the right word, "overwhelming," he continued.

"I don't even know how to process this. I should call my parents," Anita said.

"No, wait. Let's talk this out a little. Let's figure out what we know and don't know." Daniel motioned to the couch. "You should sit down. Let me get you some water."

Anita dropped onto the couch without even taking her winter jacket off. Daniel eyed her as he went to get some water. She appeared dazed and stared straight ahead. When he returned with the water, she barely looked at him as she took the glass. Like him earlier, her hand shook as she took a sip.

Sitting on the chair opposite her, Daniel gave her a few moments to register what was happening.

"Okay," she said finally. "Tell me what you know about this girl."

"Aahna. Her name is Aahna," Daniel said slowly.

Anita winced, and Daniel could tell that the stranger Anita showed a slight jealousy towards was now taking form as a real person.

Anita appeared to compose herself. "What part of Kolkata is Aahna from?"

Daniel scratched his head. It had been a long time, and the names had all blurred together. "Um, I honestly don't know. She told me, but the language is foreign and the name didn't resonate with me."

"Fine, how old is she," Anita continued, as if checking off an imaginary list.

Daniel paused. "Twenty-five," he said, remembering the conversation the two of them had about how her mother was upset she wasn't yet married at such an 'old' age. A wave of melancholy came over him. He hadn't had to think about Aahna in such detail for many months, and all the painful memories of leaving her were making an appearance yet again. He pushed them down, and tried to focus on answering Anita's questions.

"So that puts us at the same age," Anita said matter-of-factly. "I guess more importantly, do you know her birthday?"

"July 26th," Daniel responded automatically. Exactly seven months after his own.

"Christ."

"Are you sure yours is the right date?" Daniel pressed gently. "I mean, orphanages might not always keep the best records. Or I could imagine that whoever brought you there might not have communicated the most accurate facts about you to the staff."

"My parents told me that the staff was able to confirm that I was only a day old when I was brought there. That date was July 27th, 1988." Anita paused. "Someone really didn't want me," she said with a gentle but pained smile.

Daniel placed a hand on hers. The texture of the skin was different, what with the climate and labor of Anita's life being drastically different than Aahna's. But the size and shape were identical. Closing his eyes, he could almost feel being back in India, sitting on a park bench away from a crowd. He shook the thought out of his head again, realizing the turmoil that was being brought up in Anita's life. He really did need to concentrate with her.

"I can appreciate how hard this is for you," Daniel said. "Take all the time you need." He patted her hand and then moved it away. "What else do you want to know?" he said kindly. "About your sister," he added as an afterthought.

It took only that one word for tears to form in Anita's eyes. She rested her head in her hands and sniffed. There was no sobbing. Only quiet crying, as the realization of what was being said appeared to be taking effect. After a few moments, she finally raised her face.

"Could you tell me about her?" she asked quietly. "What you liked about her?"

Daniel smiled. "How much time do you have?"

Anita smiled through her tears. "One more question, did you ever meet...," Anita looked up at the ceiling, as if garnering strength, "my mother?" she finished.

"No. I assume I would have been shipped back to Canada much sooner if I had," he said, trying to keep the mood light, as impossible as that seemed in the moment. "Not that she was mean," he quickly corrected. "I think she was just really protective of Aahna."

Anita nodded. "I'm sure she just wanted the best for her. Although I'm surprised. I would think most middle-class families wouldn't mind their daughter falling for a good-looking foreigner with a respectable job."

Daniel stared straight ahead, realizing that in all of their chatter, he had unintentionally forgotten to tell Anita one major element of Aahna and her family. Rubbing his forehead with his hands, he realized how much more complicated this already delicate conversation was going to become.

"She's actually not middle-class," Daniel started slowly. "Aahna and her family are part of a lower caste."

"How much lower?"

"She was a maid. A cleaning lady in the office where I worked." Daniel tried to not look at Anita's reaction, anticipating what it would be. He knew Anita had been to India several times with her family, and that was she well-versed in how the caste system worked. Like all middle-class families, he assumed her family in India had more than one maid in their employ. The status difference would be that much greater to a person like her, who had been brought up to accept it and never question the roles of individuals who came in and out of her relatives' homes.

"My head is pounding," Anita said.

"Tell me about it."

"I feel really tired all of a sudden."

"I totally understand. You can lie down here, or in my room. Whatever you want."

Anita rested her head back onto the couch. "I don't even know how I'm supposed to tell my parents. They probably never knew anything about my real family."

"Probably not. Especially since they brought you to Canada."

"I should really talk to them," she said.

"Wait until tomorrow. I think you should really get some rest tonight. Honestly, just stay here on the couch. It's late. I'll get you a blanket and a pillow." Daniel patted her knee as he got up. "And maybe, you want to take your jacket off." He smiled at her, but she didn't look at him.

Heading towards the linen closet, he heard her shift around on the couch. "Once I tell my parents, I think I have to go to India," he heard her call out to him.

Daniel appeared back in the living room holding a fleece blanket and a down pillow. "If that's what you really want," he said.

"And you're going to come with me."

Chapter Twelve

The files were piling up on the wooden desk that belonged to Sunil in his corner office. Even in this age of technology, so many things were still printed out, stuffed into folders and abandoned on Sunil's desk for reasons unbeknownst to him. He had just stepped into the office on that warm October morning and he knew he was already behind in his emails. The work seemed never ending and he was surprised his controlling wife hadn't yet shared her opinion on the matter.

They had already gotten into an argument earlier that morning about their son's schooling. Moumita wanted to hire more tutors, to give her son an edge, while Sunil had wanted to allow him to enjoy his already fleeting childhood. The school years were intensely fierce for children from an early age, forcing most to abandon any extra-curricular activities in favor of lengthy and numerous tutorial sessions. All of this for a chance at a semi-prestigious post-secondary school, and all of it started at the tender age that Sunil's son now had the pleasure of being.

As he flipped through a handful of files, Sunil acknowledged unhappily how the race that was life was never really ending. He was still in the heart of it, wondering if he would get the next promotion or even if his boss noticed the work he did. He was fortunate enough that his childhood years had been far more enjoyable than what his son was going to go through. And he prepared himself for the inevitability of his son burning out at a young age. Sunil tossed the files back onto his desk and focused on his computer. Only thirty-eight new emails since the previous day, not including the ones he hadn't gotten to from the week before. Sighing, he stretched his arms to get rejuvenated, rolled his neck a couple of times and finally put his hand on the mouse.   He scanned through the most recent emails first, mentally prioritizing the subject lines in his head. Most were ones that would require further analysis and brain power, something he had no desire of exercising right in that moment. He closed his eyes for a second and thought about early retirement. He quickly realized the futility of that dream and continued sifting through his emails. As he went down the list, a new one popped up on his screen. Normally he wouldn't get distracted by new emails but the name caught his eye. It was a sender he hadn't spoken to in quite some time.

"Daniel," he whispered to himself. Knowing that there were no mutual projects between their offices at the moment, Sunil's curiosity forced him to abandon his other work and quickly open up the correspondence.

He skimmed over the first few lines which consisted of the usual pleasantries and small talk. It was the next paragraph that caught his eye and stopped him cold. Key phrases began to jump out at him.

Daniel returning to India.

Ruma putting a child up for adoption.

Aahna having a twin.

It all seemed so implausible and surreal. Sunil read the paragraph three times before processing the news. The email ended simply.

"I understand you must be surprised, but this is obviously a delicate matter. I would need your discretion, and most importantly, we would need your help to come into contact with Aahna. Rest assured I have no plans to interfere in her life. This visit is merely to help a friend and the situation supersedes any values you or I may disagree on. I will be in the country for only a week, and I hope that I can count on your help. It will make things smoother if Aahna has a trusted person by her side as she hears of this news. I look forward to your reply. Regards, Daniel."

Sunil leaned back in his chair after finishing the email. The news left him stunned. He couldn't imagine how Aahna and her family would react. Daniel was right. As much as Sunil didn't want him back in Aahna's life, this was beyond any petty disagreements.

For a second he contemplated telling Aahna and her family first. He had known them for years and didn't want them to be blindsided. But it was this other girl's decision, he supposed.   This girl Anita, who, according to the email had confirmed with her adopted parents that there was potential legitimacy of the situation. They had called the orphanage but to no avail, as most of the staff had long since left in the past twenty-five years. A fire ten years prior had caused the majority of records to be expunged, although Sunil had no confidence in the types of records that were stored there in the first place. Anita was willing to come to India directly and confront Ruma, armed with only a birthdate and identical features as evidence.

Thinking about it longer, Sunil couldn't blame her. He would most likely go to all lengths to find out the truth about a past he thought he knew. It also wasn't Sunil's place to dictate the conditions of the meeting. Therefore, he knew he could only do as Daniel asked.

Sunil leaned out of his office and called out his secretary's name.

"Yes sir," the young employee said hurrying into her boss's office.

"Cancel my afternoon next Monday." Sunil glanced at his computer. "I'll need to pick up an old colleague and his friend from the airport."

Chapter Thirteen

The flight attendant leaned over Daniel to hand Anita her tomato juice and pretzels. He was a man in his thirties with wavy black hair and slightly crooked teeth, and as he passed Anita a napkin, Daniel wondered what the life of a flight attendant was really like. Travelling to all parts of the world was certainly fascinating, but spending the better of your life walking up and down a cramped hallway with hundreds of people staring at you daily hardly seemed worth it. He counted up the amount of air miles he had accumulated in the last year from all of his travels, and couldn't believe he was taking a trip back to India in a matter of months.

Sipping on his soft drink, he looked over at Anita. She was staring out the window, having not said much since they boarded the flight. He wanted to give her some space, but it was a twenty-two hour flight plus a layover in England. He was going to lose his own sanity if she didn't converse with him soon. The in-flight magazine provided some light reading for ten minutes, but Daniel found himself bored quickly. As he started to channel surf on the personal T.V., Anita finally turned in his direction.

"I just realized how bittersweet this must be for you," she said, leaning her head back and watching him closely.

"You shouldn't think about me," he responded. "This is a monumental trip you're on right now. That's got to be your focus."

Daniel pushed the recline button on his chair and it jolted back. "How come your parents didn't end up coming?"

"They wanted to, but after I thought about it some more it dawned on me that this is going to be difficult enough for everyone. Maybe with less people and one less family dynamic to worry about, it could go smoother."

"Do you really believe that?"

Anita shrugged. "I have to believe in something."

Daniel, not sure how to respond, gazed out of Anita's window now. Having been focused on her plight, he hadn't spent too much time thinking about what the situation would be like between him and Aahna when he arrived. Paul had thought it was unwise for him to return to India. Sensibly, he had suggested that Anita should be escorted by only her family, and not by someone who had his own emotional baggage to deal with.

The evening sky began to darken as Daniel sat quietly, lost in his personal torment.

"I'm sorry things didn't work out between you two," Anita piped up. "But you have to admit that if there was ever a case of everything happening for a reason, this is it."

Daniel stared at Anita for a long time. He took in the long eyelashes that framed the darkest eyes he had ever seen. Staring into them for too long meant losing yourself in an abyss of night. Her face was small, but incredibly animated. With both Aahna and Anita, he had witnessed random bystanders glancing over when they were in the middle of telling an involved story.

"You think I'm not meant to be with her," Daniel said finally.

"I don't actually," Anita responded matter-of-factly. "If you had stayed there, you wouldn't have met me. This whole situation isn't just some peculiar coincidence. You're going to be responsible for bringing a family together after twenty-five years. Do you know how incredible that is?"

Daniel couldn't argue with that. "I'm genuinely happy for you. I really am. Adopted kids don't often get to meet their real families, especially from halfway across the world." Daniel paused. "I just don't like how I left things with her."

"As hard as everything was for you, it would have been a thousand times worse for her," Anita said. "You get to come back to Canada and keep dating and marry whomever you want. Someone who you really love. She's trapped in this pre-determined lifestyle and while her time with you may have been happy, I think it only made matters worse after you left."

"Are you saying this is all my fault?"

"Daniel, what was she supposed to do if a man like you approached her? Ignore you? Pretend you didn't exist?" Anita's face softened, probably realizing that her tone was reaching a harshness that wasn't helping the situation. "I know I don't know Aahna or much about your relationship with her. But I know girls. And I can bet my life that there wasn't a moment in those few months you were together that she didn't want you to just take her on a plane and leave her world behind." Anita leaned forward in the seat towards Daniel. "I can tell you're a good guy, and that you never meant any harm. But you were never going to bring her back to Canada were you? And even if you were honest from the beginning, there was nothing you could do to stop her from thinking it anyway. It's what we girls do," Anita smiled.

"Be delusional?"

"No. Hope."

Daniel shifted in his seat, wondering if Anita was bringing all this up to get her mind off of her own current crisis. Or maybe there was a hint of sisterly protection in her voice. Either way, she was looking at his life far too pragmatically. She echoed Paul's sentiments almost perfectly, but it was so easy to preach on paper.

They hadn't been swept up in the charm and wit of a simple girl from a small village. They hadn't watched as she proudly re-told the history of her city's most famous landmarks, or how she navigated through the city with a confidence that he hadn't yet achieved. They didn't know what it felt like when her skin brushed against his, a spark that even after countless nights with different women hadn't been extinguished. They weren't the ones in love with her. Daniel felt like banging his head against the seat in front of him. What was he thinking, heading back there? Was he going to just waltz in and pretend that everything was normal? And after the shock of having a sister would wear off, wouldn't Aahna assume that Daniel had found the perfect replacement in Anita? Paul certainly seemed to think so.

At thirty-thousand feet in the year, Daniel slowly felt the inklings of a panic attack. His breathing became jagged and he could feel his heart beating through his shirt. He blinked his eyes a few times to gain some form of control.

Anita looked at him curiously. "Are you okay?" she whispered.

Daniel rubbed his face aggressively with his hands, and then took another sip of his drink. It seemed to calm him down somewhat. He placed his elbows on the tray in front of him and rested his head in his palms, looking at Anita.

"I should make things right," he said, more to himself then to her.

"I know I asked you to come with me, and I know you're already sitting on the plane. But if, for any reason, you don't want to come with me to see her, I completely understand. More so for her sake, I can go by myself, or with your friend. I really won't mind."

"No, no," Daniel mustered. "I'm taking you there. I'll get it together before that. I promise. It's been almost eight months. I'm over this, I swear."

"Who are you trying to convince?" Anita asked kindly.

Daniel laughed. His breathing returned to normal and he leaned back in his chair. After a few moments, he looked at his travel partner. "I'm really jealous of you, do you know that?"

"No, why?" Anita asked distractedly as she leafed through her purse.

"Because starting tomorrow, she gets to be a part of your life."

***

For days Anita had wondered how she would feel landing once again in her homeland of India. This was actually the first time she had come to the country without her parents. Even at the age of twenty-five her parents felt that she was not yet ready to peruse the daunting, complex country by herself, although thousands of tourists who had never set foot there before seemed perfectly capable. She wasn't worried or nervous about arriving in India by any means. All of her relatives had been notified, although they were against her reason for the visit. Most thought that she should let sleeping dogs lie. Others who always thought the worst in people assumed that her poor biological family would attempt to extort money from her.

Anita didn't care for any of it. From the moment that her and Daniel had pieced together her past, she only had one notion. To meet her twin. Having known she was adopted from an early age, she had slowly developed a curiosity about this other family over time. She had never expected to have a twin though, and she wasn't mentally prepared to have the knowledge about her family thrown on her lap suddenly. Anita had assumed she would have to dig around and slowly uncover the truth. It was the idea of a twin that had hit her the hardest.

To learn that there was an entire being out there who was her exact duplicate had introduced an overwhelming feeling in her. And now, after weeks of conversations, tears and begging her boss for time off, she had finally arrived in her twin's city.

Daniel had informed her that she had a brother as well, and Anita, having been an only child, was excited to learn of not one but two siblings. She hadn't quite figured out how she would continue a relationship with her new family, but her parents had encouraged her to take one step at a time.

It was Daniel's co-worker who had picked the two of them up at the airport. She was now seated in his backseat as the car whizzed in and out of traffic, stopping and starting at what would seem like to an outsider, arbitrarily. The air had been humid when they landed, and the familiar sights and smells had brought Anita back to the many times she had been here. Nearly eight years had passed since the last visit, but Anita could remember each detail about the city and its people, her people.

Sunil seemed like a nice man. She conversed with him in Bengali for a few minutes and then both had switched back to English for Daniel's sake. Anita ignored Sunil's initial gasp when they first saw each other, realizing he probably didn't believe the twin factor until that moment. She still caught him staring through the rearview mirror with a look of disbelief. In the car, Daniel brought Sunil up to speed on how they had come to meet and Anita used that time to gaze out the window. She tried to pinpoint the differences from all of her previous visits, starting at the tender age of four. There were more skyscrapers and flyovers, and the city seemed overrun with even more people, a fact that Anita had a hard time fathoming since she already found it too populated. She closed her eyes, the exhaustion from the journey final overtaking her, and thought about the plan the three of them had come up with for meeting her family. Sunil had suggested that Anita arrive at his apartment the next morning, prior to Aahna's shift and meet her there. All three had agreed that it would be Sunil to break the news to Aahna. He had known her the longest and the best, and anything Daniel would say to Aahna would be laced with extra drama and history. Anita was originally disappointed that Daniel had come to the decision to not be in the apartment during the initial exchange. His presence would only distract from the real purpose of the visit, and Anita had finally agreed. She had to accept the fact that theirs was a story that she wasn't privy to, and she would have to let Daniel and Aahna figure out how to proceed in their own time.

The car arrived at the hotel and after Sunil promised to pick her up the next morning, they bid their farewells for the evening and with one last obvious look of disbelief, Sunil drove off.

"You didn't want to stay with your relatives?" Daniel asked as they pulled their luggage into the foyer.

"No. They'd try and talk me out of everything. I need to sort things out on my own and deal with tomorrow's outcome without their input," Anita replied. "Besides, I couldn't leave you alone. I dragged you all the way here." Making plans for dinner later, the two separated on their respective hotel floors after checking in.

In all of her visits to India, Anita had never actually stayed in a hotel. Their relatives' houses were always the one and only stop for hospitality, and while she would miss their company, she was relieved for the peace and quiet of the small hotel room. It consisted of a double bed and small desk in the corner, with a medium sized window overlooking the parking lot. She peered into the washroom, expecting the worst. For all of the modern conveniences and strides India had made, the washroom upgrade never seemed to be on its list. Anita was relieved to find a western style washroom, equipped with a modern toilet, bathtub and ceramic sink.

She water felt nice and cool as she washed her face and hands after the long trip. Anita stared into the mirror for a long time, realizing how odd it was going to be to see someone else with the same face. She hadn't even come up with any talking points, assuming the two would sit together in shock for the majority of the initial visit.

She headed back into the bedroom and plopped down onto the bed. After texting her parents about her safe arrival, she rolled over and stared at the wall of the hotel. The flowery wallpaper was peeling in the corners and the baseboards were lined with dust and lint that had obviously not been cleaned in a while. Having been focused so much on the idea of having a twin, she hadn't stopped to think properly about the idea of meeting her biological mother. She had no idea how to handle this truth, choosing to ignore it instead. But after tomorrow, the truth would become reality and she would have no choice but to accept her lineage for everything that it was.

She rolled onto her back and stared at the ceiling, wondering if Daniel was struggling in his own room but with different emotions. Anita made a mental note to make sure they would end up eating dinner at a place that served alcohol. With the magnitude of tomorrow creeping up on them slowly, they were going to need all the help they could get.

Chapter Fourteen

Time seemed to drag on for Aahna. Each day was excruciatingly longer than the previous. And yet she trudged on, slowly accepting her lot in life. Sourav's marriage was officially fixed now, and in one month's time a new girl would arrive into their home, to take care of him and help him start a new family.

Aahna knew it was only a matter of time that it would be her turn. She had resisted long enough. But she was twenty-five now, and in her world, that was far too old for a non-educated girl like herself to be unmarried. Aahna tried not to spend too much time thinking about what was coming up in her life. Her focus right now was on her mother's health and her brother's wedding. And yet sometimes, in the distance, she would hear a voice in her head, of someone saying her name. She hoped she would hear that voice forever, if only to provide exhilaration in an otherwise banal life.

That October morning started off no differently than any of the others that had come before it. Knocking on Sunil's door, Aahna waited patiently for Moumita to answer it and dictate her usual orders. She was surprised to see Sunil himself answer the door. He was already dressed for work, in his usual button down dress shirt and suit pants. But to Aahna, he appeared almost nervous, as if seeing her for the first time.

She paused in the doorway, unsure if she should take the first step or wait him for him to ask her in. When Sunil didn't say anything, Aahna started to speak, "Can I come in Sir? Is everything okay?"

Hearing her voice seemed to draw Sunil out of his daze, and he nodded quickly and opened the door wider.

"Didi is not here today?" Aahna asked, referring to Moumita.

"I asked her to step out this morning," Sunil said, his voice quavering slightly. He stood still in the living room, making no move to continue getting ready for work.

Aahna gazed at him curiously. What was going on, she wondered.

"We have to talk," he finally said, motioning to the couch.

Aahna raised an eyebrow. Intrigued she sat down and hoped that the news was nothing about her actual job, either here or at his office.

He sat down next to her and almost immediately stood back up. "Can I get you some tea?"

Aahna shook her head, causing him to sit back down again, his hands wringing slightly.

"Sir, really is everything okay?"

Sunil took a deep breath. He glanced towards a room in the back of the apartment. The door was closed which Aahna found odd since she was required to clean the entire apartment shortly. Ignoring this, she turned her attention back to Sunil, who in turn, finally looked at her.

"Aahna, I'm about to tell you something that is going to come as a deep shock to you I believe. I know it certainly did to me."

Now it was Aahna's turn to feel nervous. She had never seen Sunil this serious before, not even when the situation with Daniel had arisen. He was always calm in her presence, a stoic figure that made her feel safe. She nodded slightly, to encourage him to continue with his news.

He breathed in again. "Aahna, did you know that your parents had given a child up for adoption many years ago?" He looked at her closely, as if gauging her reaction.

Aahna's stomach started to feel queasy and she felt her face becoming warm. This wasn't the news at all that she was expecting, and Sunil was right; deep shock was setting in slowly.

"No," she managed to muster. "Why do you think this?"

"I have proof that twenty-five years ago, they gave up a newborn girl to an orphanage here in Kolkata."

"Twenty-five years ago? That's impossible. I was born twenty-five years ago."

Sunil didn't say anything to her, but instead continued to watch her with an almost sympathetic expression.

She let his words sink in. Was he implying..? It wasn't possible. He had gotten his facts mixed up.

"You are mistaken," she finally said. "I do not know where you heard this from, but it is wrong. And I should really get to work Sir. I have another house to clean after yours." Aahna began to get up from the sofa, but Sunil gently reached out for her hand.

"Aahna, please listen to me," he said softly, pulling her back down next to him. "It would appear you have a twin sister," he finished.

Aahna stared at him, looking at all of the nuances of his face, the wrinkles near his eyes, the black mole by his jaw, the sporadic eyebrows. Rather than process the news, she focused on his features, because they made sense to her. What was coming out of his mouth didn't. Aahna shook her head.

"You are mistaken," she repeated, this time with more urgency.

"I understand this is difficult, but I promise it is true."

Sunil continued to speak, but to Aahna, his voice became hazier and hazier the more he spoke. Aahna looked down at the ground, trying to handle the news that he had just delivered. It really didn't make any sense. She had a twin sister? How was that conceivable? She had only seen this type of story on the silly television shows that were on in the houses that she cleaned. They were unrealistic and nonsensical and the fact that Sunil could imply her life was about to become as absurd seemed entirely out of character for him. Was he telling her the truth?

"How do you know this? Who has told you this?" she asked. Her voice was barely audible now, and slight tears were forming in her eyes. I will not cry, she told herself angrily. She wasn't even sure what the tears were for.

Sunil appeared uncomfortable now. He shifted in his chair and looked away from her.

"Sir?" she said. "Who has told you this?" Her voice was firm now. If this was in fact true, she was going to get the answers she needed.

"Aahna," he started to say, his voice barely above a whisper. "Daniel told me."

As if the news of a sister wasn't daunting enough, it was all Aahna could do to not gasp when Daniel's name was mentioned. The name that had been on her lips for all of these months had now been spoken aloud. And with that name came all of the memories, and all of the pain in one fluid motion. She had managed to continue living in her world, if only because he no longer existed in it in a physical sense. But there was his name, turning him once again into a flesh and bone being, a reminder that he was at one point, a part of her life.

She still didn't understand the association between him and her sister, so she sat and listened intently as Sunil explained the story.

Her eyes grew wider and wider as he repeated everything Daniel had apparently told him. She was supposed to believe that in a planet of seven billion people, he had been the one to meet two sisters who had spent their lives thousands of miles apart. Aahna didn't know what to make of any of it, and the news was weakening her by the second. When Sunil was finished he headed into the kitchen and returned with a glass of water. She sipped it slowly, still contemplating everything he had just told her.

"Daniel thinks we look alike, and that is enough proof that she is my sister?" Aahna said, the glass shaking slowly in her hands.

"Daniel isn't the only one who has seen her," Sunil said. He looked away again, clearly hiding something.

"You still have not told me everything have you?"

"There is one final piece," he said, and this time he nodded towards the closed door. Aahna followed his gaze to the door, realizing in one millisecond what, actually who, was behind it.

She let out a slow breath.

"Her name is Anita, and she has traveled really far to meet you," Sunil said. With that, he got up from the couch and headed to the door.

Aahna grasped onto the arm of the couch with her left hand and held on tight. The glass in her hand shook even more and she had to place it on the table for fear of spilling. Her body felt paralyzed as Sunil knocked on the door softly. As if in slow motion, it opened and Aahna could see a figure emerge. Sunil was blocking her view, but when he stepped aside, Aahna didn't even hesitate for a second before she gulped hard and fast. Standing only twenty-feet away from her was a petite girl, with black hair and a dark skin tone. The girl was staring at Aahna with her mouth slightly open, and she appeared hesitant as she made a motion to walk closer.

The clothes were different and her hair was layered in a style Aahna had only seen in magazines, but for all intents and purposes, Aahna knew she was looking at her own reflection. There was no denying the truth now. Sunil and Daniel had been right, and although she still didn't understand everything about the situation of the past, Aahna took a moment to bask in the sheer wonderment of the present.

"I don't know what to say," the girl spoke up. The voice was similar, but the accent was exactly like Daniel's. They were standing face to face now, two identical creatures with two entirely different histories.

"I'll give you girls some time to get to know each other," Sunil said, as he put on his shoes and headed out the door.

Aahna looked at her sister curiously. She took in the carefully lined eyes and the light pink lipstick. Her complexion was slightly lighter than Aahna's, having not spent her life in a tropical climate Aahna assumed. This is what I would look like in your world, Aahna thought. In Daniel's world.

"We should sit," Anita said. "We have a lot to catch up on," she smiled.

It was Aahna's smile, through and through. The structure of her teeth was different, as was the shade of white. But the mouth was the same, and her cheeks rose to the exact same level when she smiled.

Aahna sat down carefully on the couch next to her. "Yes, yes we do." Aahna took a long deep breath and she felt herself relax. It had only been a few minutes but already she felt a connection. The connection of being in the presence of one of your own. Aahna stared into her own eyes. "And after we catch up," Aahna continued, "you will want to meet our mother."

***

Daniel paced back and forth in the hotel lobby. He was supposed to meet Anita at noon for lunch, and more importantly for a recap of that day's events. He checked his watch nervously hoping everything had gone smoothly that day.

Daniel had spent the morning at the TargetLife office. Having not been able to convince his boss for an impromptu one-week vacation, they had compromised that he could leave the country provided he worked from the Kolkata office. But now he was on his hour lunch and Anita was already fifteen minutes late. Sunil had shown up at the office at his usual time, and informed Daniel that the two sisters had in fact met, but was unable to provide any further information. He had left the girls in his apartment, trusting Anita with a key to lock up when the reunion was over. Trying to hide his slight annoyance at Sunil's nonchalant demeanor, Daniel had attempted to work all morning, but three hours later couldn't produce a single work product.

Now he was stuck at the hotel pacing, ignoring the staff as they watched him almost amused. Trying her cell phone for the third time but to no avail, Daniel contemplated heading back into the office. Anything was better than just waiting around without any information.

He was about to head out the door when a large white taxi pulled up the driveway and Anita jumped out of it.

"I'm so sorry," she exclaimed out of breath, while tossing rupees at the cab driver. She said something to him in her native Bengali causing him to nod and drove off. Hoisting her purse on to her shoulder she grabbed Daniel's hand and pulled him back into the lobby.

"Did you eat?" she asked, still breathless.

"Who cares?" Daniel exclaimed. This time he grabbed her sleeve and took her to a corner of the lobby where two arm chairs sat facing each other. Just like our first date, he mused for a second, but re-focused quickly.

"Sit down," he ordered. "Tell me what happened!"

Throwing her bag onto the floor, Anita sat down with an excited expression on her face.   "I need water," she said.

"Are you trying to kill me?" Daniel responded.

"Okay, okay," she said smiling. "It was amazing. Honestly, I couldn't have asked it to go better."

Daniel sat back relieved. "Oh Anita, I'm so happy for you. I really am." His tone was genuine and sincere.

"I met her."

"You met Aahna. I know."

"No, I mean, yes. But I meant, I met my mother." Tears formed in Anita's eyes almost immediately, as if the morning's events had finally sunk in. "That's why I was late. The cab got lost coming back from her house."

"You went to her house?" Daniel said incredulously, referring of course to no one else except Aahna.

"Yes. Aahna took me there after we left Sunil's apartment. She didn't want me to wait any longer. Oh Daniel, she seemed over the moon about everything. I thought maybe she would be hesitant at first, and maybe she wouldn't want me to meet her mother. I mean, our mother." Anita paused, appearing lost in her thoughts for a moment.

"Tell me about meeting your mother," Daniel said gently.

"I don't know where to start," Anita said, resting her head back on the chair and looking out the nearby window. A blue luxury car drove up, dropping off a wealthy looking Indian couple wearing western clothes. The woman walked through the doors, ignoring the young bellhop who opened the door for her, as if rudeness was the ultimate display of prosperity. Daniel and Anita's gaze followed the woman and her partner all the way from the lobby to the elevators. When they disappeared from view, Daniel turned to face Anita again.

"Start at the beginning," he prodded nicely.

"Their house...it's so small...," Anita's voice trailed off. "I knew they were poor, but if you could see it."

Daniel felt a pang of guilt. Aahna's house. She had never spoken of her home in all of their conversations. And knowing it might be a delicate topic, Daniel had also steered clear of it. If he had even given her one iota of hope that she could leave her surroundings, it was one iota too many. A wave of sadness washed over him. He was so close to her right now, but had never felt so removed from her world. Even after spending so much time with her in their months together, he had often forgotten about her plight. She had hid it well, he thought. But Daniel should have known better. Not wanting to hear anything more about the house out of pure guilt, Daniel steered Anita back to discussing her mother.

"She looks like her son, my brother. I saw a picture of him, but he was at work and so I guess I'll meet him later. Aahna said we look like our father. Daniel, when I walked into that house and saw my mother... I can't even explain it properly. First she looked like she saw a ghost. And then her face melted. I don't think any of us could see anything properly after that because we were all just sobbing." Anita dabbed the corners of her eyes with her sleeves at the memory.

"Did you ask her why she gave you up for adoption?"

"I wasn't going to, but she wanted to explain anyway. The family was so poor, and they had no idea that my mother was carrying twins. Sourav was already born, so the expectation was to have only one more child. When the midwife produced two daughters, they were in shock. They knew they could barely afford having two children, let alone three." Anita looked down at her hands. "They did what they had to do," she said quietly. "I hold no ill will. I can't."

"I know you don't," Daniel said nicely. He glanced at the clock behind the receptionist's desk. "I have to go back to the office. Sunil's expecting me." He stood up and pulled Anita towards him for a hug. The frame of her body fell into him the exact same way Aahna's had. He closed his eyes. "This was it. This was the hardest part."

"I know. I'm going to go back now and spend time with them, but I'll see you for dinner?"

"Of course, take your time. You have all week with them, and then you can figure out what to do after that. Just enjoy all this now."

"Are you going to see her? Aahna, I mean?"

Daniel pulled Anita away from him, not wanting to answer the question. "I should," he said slowly. "I just haven't figured out how."

"She asked how you were doing." Anita paused. "For what it's worth, she still misses you."

"How do you know that?"

"Let's call it twin intuition," Anita said, winking.

Daniel laughed. "I guess that's an innate quality. I really do have to go. But I'll touch base with you later okay?"

Anita nodded and Daniel turned to leave.

He was almost at the door, when he heard Anita call his name. Meeting him at the door, she took a deep breath.

"What is it Anita?"

"I saw that life." There was a pained expression on her face. "That was supposed to be my life."

"You can't think of it that way. You're leading the life you're supposed to."

"But how can I just leave them in this state and go back to my fancy condo?"

"Anita, you don't have to come up with those answers now. You really need to just live in the moment and be with your family. You'll figure the rest out."

"I just keep thinking…"

"Listen to me," Daniel said, putting both hands on Anita's shoulders and looking her right in the eye. "Your parents gave you up because they realized they couldn't afford the life you deserved. That decision would have killed them then as much as this is killing you now."

"And Aahna? What does she deserve?" Anita looked up at Daniel, the tears re-appearing again.

Daniel looked away, not able to stand the sight of a woman crying. Without responding to her, Daniel pushed through the hotel door and stepped out into the bright sunlight. He knew the answer to the question Anita posed, and he cursed himself for not having the strength to make it come true.

***

Back at the office, Daniel had a difficult time concentrating. He had promised his boss he would be a productive employee during the week he was away, and in return his boss had accepted Daniel's vague request to help a friend in India without question.

It hadn't occurred to him that he could just show up in Kolkata and work nine to five diligently. The drama that was in Anita's life was only compounded by his own drama at potentially having to see Aahna. In hindsight, Daniel contemplated whether this trip was necessary for him. Anita had adjusted quickly to her new family and she had plenty of relatives in the area to provide moral support if needed. But he had almost jumped at the chance when she had proposed his company. Now that he was here, he was less than confident in his decision, and today, only his first day back in the country, he found himself hiding out at his desk, staring at his screen and processing nothing.

Not realizing how quickly time could pass just by doing nothing, he hadn't noticed that the majority of his co-workers, including Sunil had left for the day. It was just after 6pm and Daniel's stomach was beginning to growl at the same time a headache was intensifying. Jet lag had set in three hours prior and now his body was officially confused about how to feel. He rubbed his eyes and stared out the window as he had done so many times before from that same seat. The darkness of the night had already begun to set in, even though he knew the temperature was still relatively mild. Mild for him anyway; a Canadian used to harsh winters.

It was the rattle of dishes nearby that brought him out of his daze, and he realized that the cleaning staff had arrived. Time to go home, he thought to himself wearily. Anita would be expecting him soon for dinner and both of them were bound to fall asleep early tonight what with the sheer exhaustion of the day's events combined with the jet lag.

Daniel threw his laptop into its bag and grabbed his empty but stained coffee mug. Heading towards the kitchen on his way out of the office Daniel could hear the sound of water running and dishes that were clanging against the sink as someone was clearly washing them after the work day. It reminded him of how he had first met Aahna in the kitchen as she was cleaning up. He paused outside suddenly overwhelmed with the memory. He hesitated going into the kitchen and re-living that moment with some other young girl from the cleaning staff, and almost debated returning his mug to his desk and disappearing out the door. Assuming the lack of sleep was getting the better of him, he ignored this slightly panicked feeling and headed into the kitchen.

He could count on his hands the number of times he had actually gasped in his life and most of them were during a cheap thrills horror movie. He was a grown man, and gasping was designed for women who had found the perfect pair of shoes. But here he stood, a thirty-two year old man, a gasp escaping from his throat.

And there she stood, all five-feet zero inches of her. She was hunched over the sink, the sound of the water clearly preventing her from realizing someone had joined her in the kitchen. Her hair was pulled back in a bun, with wisps of it falling down her back and to the sides of her face. She was tapping her foot slightly against the cabinet and her clothes fell loosely against her petite frame.

Daniel couldn't see her face, but he didn't need to. He had seen it plenty of times in his dreams and in the back of his mind over the past eight months. He wasn't prepared for this, and almost subconsciously, he found himself stepping back. In that moment, as if the young girl at the sink sensed another presence, she finally turned around.

Overcome with only pure emotion, forgetting everything he had promised himself he wouldn't do and not caring who was left in the office, Daniel found himself closing the gap between them. Dropping his laptop bag and coffee mug in one fell swoop, he picked her up and kissed her eagerly, the way he had wanted to for so long. At first Aahna seemed resistant, but then she wrapped her arms and soapy hands around his neck and reciprocated.

After a couple of minutes they pulled away, the passion still present, but reality entering into their minds slowly. He still held onto her and they looked into each other's eyes without speaking. For the second time that day, Daniel witnessed tears forming in the same eyes, and slowly he put her back down on the ground.

"I'm sorry," he started, not sure what else to say.

Aahna nodded slightly. She wiped her eyes with her hands then turned off the sink. The sudden silence engulfed the two of them as they stood in the tiny kitchen. It was the scene of so many of their interactions, ranging from the creation of a new spark, to a comfortableness shared between old friends to the intensity of a deep, forbidden love.

She looked the same to Daniel. Only months had passed so there was no expectation of any drastic physical aging, but standing with her again, it was as if time had not befallen on them.

"How are you?" she finally said.

It was a loaded question, and he knew it. It represented so many feelings, so many moments, so much turmoil. In the end, he simply said, "I'm fine".

"I have a sister," Aahna announced suddenly, as if realizing that they shared a topic other than themselves. "And you found her. I don't know how to thank you."

"I didn't do anything," Daniel replied. "It was pure dumb luck that I met her."

"I don't know what that means, but I don't believe it was just luck. You were meant to meet us both."

"Anita said the same thing to me," he said. "Great minds I suppose."

Aahna looked confused, and Daniel remembered that he had to prevent himself from speaking in his western colloquial language. "I'm just happy you two got to meet. I can only imagine how excited you and your family must feel to be reunited."

"My mother, mostly. She had kept this secret for so many years, and she admitted feeling guilty about it all this time." Aahna paused. "She regrets that my father never met her."

Daniel nodded. "Your father knew what kind of girl you would become. I'm sure he had no regrets."

Aahna smiled, the familiar one that still made Daniel's heart skip a beat.

"Can I ask you something?" she asked, her voice growing quiet.

"Sure."

"Did you and Anita ever...," her voice trailed off.

Daniel raised an eyebrow. "No," he said almost immediately, wanting to put her innocent mind at rest. "It just never worked out. I'm not sure it was supposed to."

Aahna nodded, attempting to hide her obvious relief. "She seems lovely," Aahna continued.

"She is. And you two will spend the rest of your lives getting to know each other. Today's only the first day."

A cough was heard in the far office and Daniel remembered that there may still be other employees working late. Not wanting to get Aahna in trouble he realized it was most likely time to say goodbye, yet again.

"Actually, how come you're working here? I thought your mother made you quit after she found out about me?"

"Once you left for Canada, she didn't have a reason to stop me from coming here. It is good money, and well, she didn't want us to go back on our word to Sunil Sir." Aahna looked down at her hands. "Coming back here after you had left has been one of the hardest things I had to do. Seeing your empty desk, knowing that you wouldn't sneak up on me in the kitchen, not being able to chat with you. There are days when it is still unbearable." She didn't look up at him.

"I shouldn't have come back," Daniel said, ignoring the massive pang in his heart. "I should have let you move on."

"No," she said. "Seeing you today, even if it's under different circumstances, is something that will get me through the hard days. Thank you for that."

Daniel shook his head. "Please don't thank me." He wanted so much to stay there with her now, but the conversation was becoming difficult again and repetitive of their earlier goodbye. He knew they both couldn't handle that again. As much as the days had seemed stretched out since he had last seen her, deep down they both knew there was not enough time in the world that would heal their hearts completely.

"Aahna, I should go." Daniel picked up his laptop bag which was resting haphazardly against the wall. He edged closer to her again and kissed her lightly on the forehead. "For what it's worth," he said, "you still have my heart." With that, Daniel headed out of the kitchen for the last time.

There was no perfect pair of shoes in sight, but he could hear the gasp as he left Aahna's side and walked out the door.

Chapter Fifteen

Christmas came and went rather uneventfully this year, what with the arrival of Paul and Megan's wedding day a mere three days later. The original Harp family had a quiet dinner at home with only the upcoming nuptials as their main topic of conversation. After weeks of preparation, the Harp's household finally maintained a relaxed state. The house was now spotless, Sophia spending all of her time polishing and re-polishing the silverware. New bedding had been bought for the guestrooms and even Paul and Daniel's old rooms were stripped of trophies and old posters and replaced with a fresh coat of paint. The front and back gardens were covered in the whitest snow and Richard had spent the previous weekend dotting the front of the house with soft twinkle lights. The cozy, welcoming image of the house was complete. The family's only duty at that point was to arrive at the church on time and pick up relatives over the next few days.

It had been nearly two months since Daniel and Anita had arrived back from India. To his parents, he had visited the country under the guise of work, having no reason to explain anything further. Now that he had finally received the closure he needed, Daniel wanted to put everything about India behind him. A full year had almost passed since he first met Aahna and he still couldn't believe the emotional upheaval it had caused in his life.

Anita had understood that at least for the near future, Daniel didn't want updates on Aahna's life. He knew that she on the other hand had left India feeling jubilated about the visit with her family. Although they had initially refused to take any money from her, she had compelled them to accept enough compensation for visits to a nearby Internet café where they could all chat regularly Her original idea about setting them up with a computer and internet connection in their home was met with dismay by Sunil who had assured her that the computer would last only one day before it was stolen.

Now that Daniel counted Anita as a close friend in his life, the two spent time having coffee, going to the movies and meeting each other's friends. It was a perfectly platonic relationship, and they had settled into their roles easily. Since he had not started dating anyone new, Daniel had even requested Anita accompany him to Paul's wedding, which she graciously accepted.

The day after Christmas saw the arrival of relatives of the Harp family from out of town. Daniel and his father, Richard, spent most of the day driving back and forth from the airport to the Harp household. There was his father's brother and wife from Cleveland. David and Shirley were the closest to Daniel and Paul, living only a few hours away during their childhood allowed the families to visit each other often. A retired police officer, David was gruff but kind, and Shirley, a former nurse, had only sweetness coming out of her pores. Having no children of their own, the two had looked at Daniel and Paul as their own.

In the afternoon, Daniel's maternal aunt and uncle drove in from nearby Buffalo. Linda was quiet and reserved, having never amalgamated herself with the family. She remained clingy with her oldest daughter who was 28, but who was currently vacationing in Hawaii with her boyfriend. Bob, Sophia's brother, was the complete opposite, laughing and joking with everyone in his path. It was no secret that theirs was only a marriage of resigned convenience.

The final relative to arrive was a cousin from Miami. Grace was twenty-four, the daughter of Richard's youngest brother. He was unable to attend the wedding due to a recent surgery. Grace arrived in the evening and was Daniel's final shuttle to the airport and back to his parent's house.

He too was staying in St. Catherines during the wedding period, wanting to spend time with his relatives but selfishly needing to be surrounded by the usual family drama. Anything to keep his mind off Aahna.

***

The small banquet hall was brimming with guests when Aahna and her family arrived for Sourav's wedding. It was tastefully decorated with fresh flowers, and a small banner displaying the names of Sourav and his bride-to-be, Vidya. Chairs were lined up in front of the small carpet covered platform where the ceremony would be held. With the bride's family traditionally bearing the brunt of the cost for the wedding, Aahna was pleased that they had chosen delicate yet inexpensive décor, knowing full well that a wedding was merely a party, and that the marriage was the true event.

As Sourav made his way to the front to be seated next to the priest, Aahna took a seat in the front row with her mother. Behind her, Sunil and his family sat quietly with the other guests. He smiled at Aahna as she took her seat. Aahna glanced back at Moumita, who looked embarrassed to be attending a wedding in this neighborhood and for someone in her servant's family on top of that.   Raina and her husband Vikas were seated in the row behind Sunil. Aahna caught her friend's eye and they smiled at each other. She ignored Vikas, he being the only person she didn't want in attendance on her brother's big day.

Aahna faced the front again as the priest took Sourav through the usual groom's rituals prior to the bride's arrival. As she watched Sourav bow down in front of the ceremonial fire, Aahna wished her father could be here to witness his son's milestone with the rest of the family.

It also made her wonder about how he would have felt about Daniel, and more recently, Anita. Who would have guessed the impact that two arbitrary Canadians could have on her quiet, unassuming life. That they could enter her world and in a few short weeks, alter her complete existence. Her mother hadn't pressured her to get married since Anita had left. She had been preoccupied with Sourav's wedding, and of course, was adjusting to the notion that in her mind, her family was reunited. The news of Anita had lifted Ruma out of her health issues as well. Her chest had finally cleared up and the coughing and wheezing had subsided. It was nothing short of a miracle and a new found way of looking at life. The Roy's had wanted Anita at Sourav's wedding, but vacation time and lack of money had gotten in the way. She had promised to return soon however, for a longer trip, and this time with her own parents.

Ruma leaned towards Aahna with a somber expression on her face. "This is all I have ever wanted for you," she said. "I know you think I don't understand you, but you are your father's daughter." Aahna kept her face forward, unable to look in her mother's eyes. "You have always been stubborn and strong-willed, and although you might not believe it, I sometimes do know what's best for you. A life with a nice man who can take care of you, in our world; that is what is good for you. Your father would want you to be the best person you can be, but do not mistake that as being better than us."

The crowd began to murmur and shuffle in their seats, and Aahna knew it was time for the bride's arrival. With her mother's words ringing in her ears, she too turned in her seat and peered over the crowd to watch her future sister-in-law be carried down the aisle on a small wooden platform by four male relatives. As they passed by her, Aahna felt an overwhelming sense of joy for her brother as he embarked on this next chapter. She put all of her energy into focusing on the wedding in front of her, and the new addition to her family. Anything to keep her mind off Daniel.

***

"The wedding was great. Your family should be so happy and relieved," Anita shouted over the music, standing next to the bar with Daniel.

Daniel smiled back at her. The wedding had been great. Everything had been on time, and Megan's idea of having the reception in a heated greenhouse while the snow fell outside had turned out perfectly. Vinery twisted throughout the ceiling beams and the freshly painted wooden trellises. Tables and chairs were covered in lush white linens, with silver runners and bows providing the accents. Neutral colored Christmas lights covered the roof and the doors, and even Daniel had to admit there was a magical quality about the day. The main events were over, drunken speeches were said, food was eaten, and now the exciting portion of the evening had started. As he watched Paul and Megan dance with their friends, Daniel couldn't help but feel elated as his brother and new wife started their lives together.

"Now that your younger brother is married, your parents are going to be all over you!" Anita said, standing closely to Daniel. She was on her third glass of wine, and it was beginning to show. Daniel looked at her, more amused than anything else.

"This wedding should tie them over for a while," he answered back.

"I know you don't want to talk about it," Anita slurred, "but I think you should just to go to India and marry my sister!" Although the music was loud, a few guests at the bar looked over at the two of them with raised eyebrows.

Daniel grabbed Anita's arm and pulled her away. "You're drunk," he hissed.

"I know that. It doesn't mean what I'm saying isn't true."

"I told you I didn't want to talk about this. And today of all days?" He glared at Anita, getting more and more annoyed by the second.

"What's the big deal? If you were truly over her, you wouldn't still be upset if I brought her name up."

Daniel ignored Anita. He stared at the dance floor wondering at what point he could just leave her standing there.

"Is it her family you're worried about?" she continued.

"Can you at least keep your voice down?"

"Sorry," she said, resting her hands on the back of a chair, clearly trying to maintain her balance. "I'm just saying, you brought their daughter and sister back into their lives after twenty-five years. Our mother believes entirely in fate, and you sir, could buy up their entire neighborhood and turn it into a mini-mall and they still wouldn't be upset."

Daniel looked at his drunken friend.

"They're probably building a shrine of you as we speak."

"Would you please stop?" he finally said. "Aren't there any guys here that you're interested in? I will happily introduce them to the drunken version of you."

"Okay, okay," Anita said, putting both hands up and stepping backwards. "I've said my piece. If you need me, I'll be on the dance floor doing my thing."

Daniel rolled his eyes but couldn't help but laugh at the same time. He watched as she fumbled her way past other guests and jumped in front of Paul and Megan as a popular song started playing. She fumbled past Richard who was heading towards Daniel. Bracing himself for the second lecture in a matter of moments, Daniel was surprised to see Richard smiling loudly.

"Danny boy," Richard exclaimed heartily, slapping his oldest son on the back. Apparently Anita wasn't the only one who had made friends with the bartender. "Why are you standing here all by yourself? You should be joining the party!" The drink in Richard's hand spilled slightly as he leaned in far too close to Daniel.

"I'm enjoying watching others have fun," he replied.

"You see," Richard yelled. "That's always been your problem." Spittle flew from his mouth as he steadied himself using a nearby chair. "People who know what they want just go after it. That's how they become happy. You think they just sit around waiting for happiness to find them. Tell me Daniel. What will finally make you happy?"

Daniel stared at his father. The words were on the tip of his tongue. This was it, he thought. The moment where he could finally be honest with his father. The situation practically called for it. But he hesitated for a moment too long.

Richard gulped down the remainder of his drink and shook his head. "I respect you Daniel, but you've always been shy about big decisions. You're happier watching others around you live their lives, and you're just there on the outskirts of it all."

Daniel stood silent, taken aback at the outpouring of revelations from his inebriated father. He couldn't argue though. Deep down, he knew it was all true.

"If it isn't easy, you find an excuse to run. Stop running Daniel." Richard put his glass down on the table and spread his arms wide. "It's time to join the party." With that, the head of the Harp family attempted to walk in a dignified manner towards his wife.

Daniel tried to ignore everything his father just said, but even with the heavy bass pounding all around him and the distracting lyrics coming from the speakers, it was his words that rang the loudest.

***

"This food is delicious," Sunil said as Aahna approached him later.

"I'm glad you like it. The caterer is a friend of Vidya's mother."

Sunil took a spoonful of rice and fish curry and shoved it into his mouth. When he finished chewing, he continued talking. "So, a new sister and a new sister-in-law in just a matter of months. That's quite the turn of events for you and your family."

"Yes, it is an interesting period for us. But these are all happy events. I have nothing to complain about."

"Indeed," Sunil said, mixing more of his food together in expert fashion. "And what are we going to do with you?"

Aahna stared across the hall at her brother and new wife. "I don't see the point in trying to guess," she said. "Look at everything that happened to me this year. Would anyone have predicted that?"

"I suppose not. You're going to just leave it all up to fate and let the universe lead you from now on?"

Aahna shrugged. "I've been denouncing fate my entire life. But fate is what had me work in the same building as Daniel, and fate is what brought him to Anita. Maybe I should let fate run its course on my life."

Sunil cleaned up the last few morsels of rice on his plate and threw the paper plate and spoon into a nearby garbage can. "It doesn't sound like the Aahna I've known my entire life." This time he shrugged as he walked away. Aahna watched him head towards his wife and son, a seemingly happy family. She bit her lip, thinking about what she didn't want to tell Sunil.

Fate brought Daniel to me once, she thought. Maybe it will bring him back.

Chapter Sixteen

It had been a long day for Claire. She was finishing up her ten hour shift and couldn't wait to get home and open up a bottle of wine. She had switched shifts with her co-worker Annette, who was at home mending a broken heart, and who had chosen to take a sick day rather than deal with the hundreds of people she would have otherwise come in contact with.

Claire didn't mind taking over for Annette, having dealt with her own fair share of heartaches. She would have been grateful to take the day off and hide under the covers eating ice cream, anything to soothe what seemed like never-ending pain at the time. Because of Claire's natural good looks, she never had any problem meeting men. It was keeping them around that proved to be the challenge.

Her job as a ticket agent in a major airport allowed her to meet all sorts of people, although generally she was stuck watching good looking men leave for romantic destinations with a pretty girl on their arm. Six years sitting behind the same counter and she had only managed to wrangle three dates. All had started with a drink at the airport bar, and ended with a maximum of two dates upon the suitor's arrival back into the city.

Oh well, she thought to herself. When it was time, the right man would come along. At least that's what her mother kept telling her. Or hoping was more like it.

Claire glanced at her watch, only fifteen minutes left in her shift. Hopefully the last few customers would be easy to deal with. She looked at the long lineup and a family of four headed in her direction. There were seven large suitcases between them. Claire had worked at the airport long enough to know that her last fifteen minutes of the day would be saddled watching these customers move their items from one suitcase to another as they attempted to meet the weight requirements. Why people can't just weigh things at home I'll never understand, she thought.

As the family headed towards her, Claire found her eyes wandering to a gorgeous, blond man standing a few spots back in the line. He was tall and dressed impeccably, with wavy hair and blue eyes so bright, Claire could see them clearly from her spot at the counter. Please let him come to my line, she almost whispered to herself. Maybe he could be lucky date number four.

As she greeted the family and began entering their passport information into the system, she wondered about the handsome stranger in line. He had two large suitcases with him, which meant he was unlike the other business men that she normally saw travelling. Well maybe it's just a longer trip she pondered. Hmm, longer trip meant he wouldn't be back in the city for quite some time. For that matter, how could she even be sure that he was from the city and wasn't in fact heading home to some other country? She pushed the thought out of her mind, still hoping that fate would intervene and her counter would open up just as he approached the first spot in line.

As luck would have it, the family of four was quite well organized. All suitcases met the proper restrictions and there was no shuffling around for documentation. Within minutes, Claire found herself printing out their boarding passes and wishing them a safe journey. Out of the corner of her eye she saw two more passengers head to different counters just as the family departed from hers. As if on cue, the gentleman saw the opening and walked over casually to her counter.

Claire subconsciously ran her hand through her hair, hoping to smooth out any frizz and provide a neat appearance. Before she could flash her usual winning smile, he beat her to it. Happy to be seated so that he couldn't sense her knees becoming weak, she nodded at him and opened up the passport that he had slid across the counter. No ring, she thought. Please be local she said in her head, scanning the picture and the passport issue location. Toronto! Two for two. She smiled up at him, her relief showing all over her face.

"Hello, Mr. Harp," she said politely, reading his passport. "Where are we headed today?"

He shifted from his left foot to his right foot. "India," he answered matter-of-factly.

Claire looked up in surprise. There was an answer she was not expecting. Trying not to appear crestfallen she distracted herself by asking him to put his suitcases onto the weight machine.

"India," she said in an attempt to appear cool and casual. "That's quite the vacation spot."

The man chuckled, his perfectly straight white teeth making an appearance. "I wouldn't call it a vacation."

"Oh of course," Claire corrected herself. "You must be going there for work."

"I wouldn't say that either," he said, appearing coy.

Claire looked at the gorgeous stranger quizzically. If he was some doctor going there to save lives Claire was tempted to jump over the counter and ask him to marry her right there.

"Well then, Mr. Harp," she responded, in her own coy fashion. "What is a good-looking man like yourself headed to a third-world country for?"

"It's called a developing country," he answered smoothly.

Claire didn't even feel ashamed at her misnomer, wishing she could watch his mouth move forever.

"You didn't answer my question," she said in her most flirty voice.

The man paused and appeared to be choosing his next words carefully. "Have you ever met someone that you would be willing to change your entire life for?"

No, she thought, but I'm beginning to think I can.

"I'm going to start a new chapter in my life."

This does not sound promising, Claire thought. Trying not to sigh, she gave up any more flirtations and continued processing the flight. The name Daniel appeared on her screen. That's a nice name, she thought. As the flight information appeared in front of her, she raised an eyebrow.

"Sir, there seems to be some kind of error with your flight."

"Oh?" Daniel cocked his head to one side.

"There's only information here going to Kolkata, India, but there is no return flight."

Daniel smiled. "That's intentional," he said finally.

Claire was taken aback. "You're moving to India?" she asked incredulously, acting like she had known Daniel her entire life and was now questioning all of his life decisions.

Daniel shrugged, as if he has already had this conversation many times prior. "Fate can only take you so far, and then after that, you'll need the help of a ticket agent to get you there the rest of the way." He winked at Claire.

"She must be something special," Claire said quietly, all hopes of a potential relationship vanishing. The printer whirred with the sound of the boarding passes and she placed them onto the counter.

"Aahna would tell you that she's not, but I plan to spend the rest of my days telling her otherwise."

Claire couldn't help but smile. "That's a pretty name."

"I just found out what it means," Daniel said, taking back his passport and boarding pass. "To exist." Daniel laughed to himself.

"Why is that so funny?" Claire asked.

"Because from the moment I met her in her world, that's all she's ever done in mine."

With that, the seemingly love-struck gentleman smiled at Claire one last time, hoisted his bag over his shoulder and walked away from the ticket counter.

www.ingramcontent.com/pod-product-compliance
Lightning Source LLC
Chambersburg PA
CBHW031243120726
47905CB00002B/707